DOCTOR WHO AND THE
SPACE WAR

THE CHANGING FACE OF DOCTOR WHO

The cover illustration of this book portrays the
third DOCTOR WHO whose physical appearance was
altered by the Time Lords when they banished him to
the planet Earth in the twentieth century

DOCTOR WHO AND THE SPACE WAR

Based on the BBC television serial *Doctor Who and the Frontier in Space* by Malcolm Hulke by arrangement with the British Broadcasting Corporation

MALCOLM HULKE

published by
WYNDHAM PUBLICATIONS

First published simultaneously in Great Britain by
Wyndham Publications Ltd, and Allan Wingate (Publishers)
Ltd, 1976

ISBN 0 426 11033 1

Target Books are published by Wyndham Publications Ltd,
123 King Street, London W6 9JG
A Howard & Wyndham Company

Printed and bound in Great Britain
by Richard Clay (The Chaucer Press) Ltd, Bungay, Suffolk

Contents

I

Link-up in Space

The year 2540.

Earth Cargo Ship C–982 slid silently through Space on its way back to Earth. Once a smart dull grey, much of its paintwork had been scorched away by countless take-offs and landings through the atmospheres of Earth and Earth's many planet colonies. The dark shape of the spaceship was relieved by lights shining from the port-holes in its blunt nose. Inside the flight deck two men sat at the controls, both dressed in scruffy space overalls, both bored with the monotony of piloting their cargo ship through millions of miles of Space.

While Hardy made a routine check of the ship's controls, the younger space pilot, Stewart, leaned back and stretched his arms. 'You know what I'd like?'

Hardy drew a tick on his controls check list. 'What?'

'A job on one of those luxury space-liners. First Officer on the Mars–Venus cruise, that'd suit me.'

Hardy continued with his work. 'You can keep it. Spit and polish, cocktail parties with the passengers . . .'

Stewart took up on Hardy's theme, but with enthusiasm. 'And a uniform with gold braid instead of these overalls, and all those beautiful space stewardesses! I'll have that any time.'

The older man put away his check list, satisfied that the spaceship's speed, direction and internal temperature were all in order. He started to pull on his safety belt. 'The way things are heading you're more likely to wind up piloting a battle cruiser.'

Stewart was quick to answer. 'There's not going to be a war.'

'Didn't you see the President on television last night? The Dragons have attacked two more of our ships. How much longer do you think we'll stand for it?' He used the slang word for Draconians. Of all the species and life forms on the millions of inhabited planets of the Milky Way Galaxy, two had become dominant—Earthmen and Draconians. Over the past century Earth and Draconia had competed to colonise other planets, until now both possessed vast empires in Space. Fortunately the two planets were far apart, in opposite 'legs' of the swirling galaxy. By tacit agreement they confined their colonising to their respective halves of the Milky Way and generally, though not always, observed an agreed frontier in Space between each other.

Stewart also pulled on his safety belt. 'I'm a born optimist. They steal a few of our cargoes, we steal a few of theirs. But it'll blow over. Neither side could afford an all-out war.' He checked the hyper-space dials. 'We're ready for the jump.'

Hardy spoke to Earth Control on the ship's transmitter. 'Cargo Ship C-982 preparing to enter hyperspace at 22.17, seven two, two thousand five hundred and forty.' He turned to Stewart. 'Let's shoot.'

Stewart touched the hyper-space lever and the spaceship leapt into speed faster than light. The sudden force riveted both men to their seats. Hardy was the first to notice the strange object spinning towards them on the monitor screen. 'You see that?' he shouted excitedly.

Stewart looked. 'What is it?'

'Dragons. They're going to attack.'

Stewart tried to get the spinning object into focus. It looked like an oblong box and was coming straight for them. At one end of the shape a blue light flashed. 'That isn't a ship. I've never seen anything like it.'

'Well, it's going to hit us, whatever it is.'

'That's their bad luck,' said Stewart. 'But better pull out of hyper-space.'

8

Hardy had already seized the microphone. 'Cargo Ship C-982, about to pull out of hyper-space now ...'

For a moment the spinning object with its flashing blue light filled the monitor screen. Then, abruptly, as the spaceship slowed, the object vanished.

'Fancy that,' said Stewart, making a young man's pretence that he hadn't been frightened. 'You'd better report it.'

'They'll never believe us,' Hardy growled. 'But you're probably right.' He spoke into the microphone. 'Cargo Ship C-982 to Earth Control. Mysterious object sighted during hyper-space transition. Object resembled large blue box with flashing light at one end. Object vanished before collision. Present whereabouts of object unknown.'

In a gloomy corner of one of the spaceship's cargo holds stood the TARDIS. It looked, as ever, like an old-fashioned London police box. But its appearance was deceptive, for the TARDIS was a highly-advanced Time and Space ship, designed and built by the Time Lords. Doctor Who, himself a Time Lord, stole his TARDIS because he desperately wanted to travel and see the wonders of the Universe. However, the one he stole had two major faults. For one thing he could never get it to go exactly where he wanted. It seemed to have a mind of its own. The other fault was that TARDISES were designed to change their appearance on arrival so as to fit in with the local background. On the Doctor's first trip the TARDIS worked well enough to make itself look like a police box, but after that its appearance never changed again.

Though small on the outside, the interior of the TARDIS was huge, a very large and modern control room with the Time and Space mechanism in the centre.

Standing now in the corner of the cargo hold, the TARDIS looked very out of place. One of the doors flung open and a pretty young woman stepped out. Jo Grant was in a flaming temper.

'I'm never going in that thing again,' she shouted back into the TARDIS.

Jo Grant had always wanted to be a lady spy, and hoped that her uncle, an important Civil Servant, would help her achieve that ambition. Instead he had her employed by UNIT, the United Nations Intelligence Taskforce, where Brigadier Lethbridge Stewart seconded her as the Doctor's general assistant because he couldn't think what else to do with her. She still wasn't used to accompanying the Doctor on his journeys through Space and Time.

The Doctor emerged from the TARDIS. 'Now then, Jo, be reasonable.' He smiled to show that being lost in Space was all part of a day's work.

She fumed, 'Honestly, only you could have a traffic accident in Space.'

'Except that we didn't,' retorted the Doctor. 'By a brilliant last minute course correction I've materialised the TARDIS inside the spaceship.'

She took in their immediate surroundings. The hold was filled with large packing cases. 'What do we do now?'

'If I'm going to get us back to Earth, I'd better find out where we are.' He turned to go back inside the TARDIS.

'But I thought we *were* on our way back to Earth?'

The Doctor paused. 'To avoid hitting this spaceship I had to make a random jump into normal Space. I can't reach a destination if I don't know where I'm starting from. So I'd better check the instruments.'

'Doctor,' said Jo, matter-of-fact, 'even when you *do* know where you're starting from, you very rarely get where we want to go.'

He looked pained. 'I try, Jo. I try.' To avoid any

further criticism the Doctor hurried back into the TARDIS.

Jo breathed a deep sigh. Then she curiously pushed back the lid of a packing case. It contained flour, plain ordinary flour. As she let some of the flour run over her fingers, a movement through the port-hole caught her attention. Jo crossed to the port-hole and looked out into the black emptiness of infinite Space. Millions of distant stars twinkled at her. The point of interest, though, was a small black spaceship, about half a mile away. It had no lights, no markings. Some instinct told Jo that this ugly black spaceship meant danger.

On the flight deck Hardy and Stewart were also watching the spaceship, on their television monitor screen.

Hardy murmured, 'Maybe it's a wreck.' There were occasional wrecks floating in Space, ships punctured by meteorites when all the crew had been killed instantly through the sudden escape of their life-supporting oxygen.

'Or maybe they need help,' said Stewart.

Hardy pulled the microphone near his lips and tuned the radio transmitter to the inter-ship emergency wavelength. 'This is Earth Cargo Ship C-982 in close proximity to you. Do you read me?'

Both men listened for a response over the flight deck's loudspeaker. There was nothing.

Hardy tried again. 'Do you read me? Are you in need of assistance?'

Again no answer.

'We'd better enter it in the log-book,' said Stewart, reaching for the records they kept on every journey. 'How would you describe it?'

Hardy said, 'Small, black spherical craft, no markings, no recognisable classification ...'

As Hardy spoke they both heard the strange rhythmic high-pitched sound coming over the loudspeaker.

The sound rose to a peak then died away. Neither man spoke while the sound lasted. When it ended they both blinked. Now as they looked at the monitor screen they could see a Draconian spaceship, a large battle cruiser bristling with heavy armament. The guns were pointing straight at them.

At the port-hole Jo also blinked when she heard the strange sound. She saw the spaceship blur in her vision, then form into a mighty ship with what might be heavy guns protruding through its hull. But the effect was only temporary. By concentrating hard and blinking her eyes rapidly, the ship resumed its original shape.

'Doctor,' she called loudly. 'Come here!'

The Doctor was already on his way. 'I think I know *where* we are, Jo, and I've got a pretty good idea about *when* ...' He stopped, realising he hadn't got her full attention. 'What's up?'

Jo pointed. 'Look out there.'

The Doctor peered through the port-hole. 'Just a spaceship,' he smiled. 'I think we're in the twenty-sixth century. Space travel is pretty routine by now.'

'That spaceship changed shape,' said Jo. 'When I heard that sound.'

'What sound? I was inside the TARDIS.' The Doctor went on with his own thoughts. 'Anyway, we'll have to find the crew of the ship we're on. I need to know the exact date for my calculations.'

But Jo wasn't listening. 'Doctor, look at that thing. It's coming straight for us!'

Hardy was staring in disbelief at the oncoming battle cruiser. 'Dragons!'

'This close to Earth?'

'They're going to attack us!'

Stewart tried to hide his fear. 'Then we fight back. How about getting the blasters?'

'I thought you said there wouldn't be war?'

'I said they'd steal some of our cargoes and we'd steal some of theirs.' Stewart swung round to the older pilot. 'Whatever I said, get the blasters. You have the authority.'

Hardy remained in his seat. 'We can't take on a battle cruiser.'

Stewart knew he looked and sounded frightened now. 'We can defend ourselves if they try to board us. For goodness' sake, Hardy, get the blasters!'

Hardy nodded. 'For what good it may do, I'll get them.' He went off down the corridor that led all the way through the length of the spaceship.

Stewart grabbed the microphone towards his mouth. 'Emergency, emergency! Earth Cargo Ship C-982 on co-ordinate 8972–6483. We are under attack by a Draconian battle cruiser of the Galaxy class, equipped with neutronic missiles. We need immediate assistance.'

The spaceship's blasters, guns that could stun or kill according to the user's adjustment, were kept in a locked metal cupboard in the main corridor. Hardy swiftly unlocked the cupboard and lifted down two of the special guns. He was about to return to the flight deck when to his astonishment a tall man with a head of tousled fair hair approached him from the cargo hold. The man was dressed in the clothes of six hundred years ago—a long velvet jacket, frilly shirt, tight trousers.

'How do you do?' said the Doctor. 'I'm sorry about this intrusion——'

As Hardy tried to gain his wits the strange rhythmic sound was heard again. Instantly the man standing before Hardy seemed to blurr and shimmer. Hardy

13

blinked and tried to concentrate his mind. He knew now that he was facing a Draconian soldier and he was frightened. The appearance of the 'Dragons' was enough to terrify any Earth person. Their shape was basically humanoid but their claw-like hands, green dragon-shaped faces and tapered ears made an awesome spectacle. The one now facing Hardy wore Draconian military uniform and carried a gun. Hardy aimed one of the blasters directly at the Draconian he believed he could see.

'Filthy Dragon,' he shouted. 'On board our ship already, are you? Drop that gun!'

The Doctor looked at Hardy, presuming rightly that the space pilot had left his senses. 'Gun? I haven't got a gun.'

Jo came running up behind the Doctor. 'I say, Doctor, don't go prowling about on your own. Wait for me——' She saw the gun pointed at the Doctor's stomach and stopped dead. 'What's happening?'

As she spoke the strange sound was repeated. To Jo's view, Hardy blurred and shimmered. Then, to her horror, he seemed to turn into a Drashig, the foul monster that she'd met on a previous journey with the Doctor. Of all the monsters Jo had encountered, the Drashig filled her with most terror.

'Doctor,' she breathed, unable to move from sheer horror, 'it's a ... Drashig.'

The Doctor shook her by the shoulders. 'Nonsense, Jo. It's a man with a gun. Pull yourself together, girl.'

The Doctor's firm grip dispelled the hypnotic effect of the sound she had heard. As she watched, the Drashig turned back into exactly what the Doctor said —a man with a gun. The man, whoever he was, seemed terrified of the Doctor, even though he was armed and the Doctor was not.

Hardy demanded, 'How many more of you have boarded us?'

'There are just the two of us,' smiled the Doctor. 'May I ask why you're behaving——'

'Shut up! Come with me!' Hardy gestured with his blaster gun.

The Doctor turned to Jo. 'Ladies first.'

She pulled a face. 'This lady's going straight back to the TARDIS.' She turned to go but the Doctor gently took her arm.

'If we don't want to get shot,' he whispered, 'we do what this gentleman says. After all, we are his guests.'

The Draconian battle cruiser now filled the monitor screen. Stewart tried to keep the terror from his voice as he spoke into the microphone.

'This is Earth Cargo Ship C-982. Situation Red Alert. Draconians about to grapple. Does anyone hear me? I repeat, they are about to lock on now!'

A clang reverberated through the spaceship. The enemy ship had made direct contact. A strong voice came over the flight deck loudspeaker, speaking with the unmistakable accent of the Draconians.

'This is the commander of the Draconian battle cruiser. We have locked on to your vessel and are about to board. If you offer any resistance you will be destroyed. Open the hatch of your air-lock.'

Stewart's heart raced. He looked round desperately, wishing Hardy would come back. To his horror he saw two Draconion soldiers entering the flight deck. They were propelled forward at gun point by Hardy.

'I found these two Dragons in the corridor,' said Hardy.

Stewart couldn't make sense of it. 'But that's impossible ... The battle cruiser's only just locked on. Didn't you feel it?'

'I don't understand either,' agreed Hardy. 'But you can't deny the evidence of your own eyes.' He pointed the blaster gun menacingly at the Doctor and Jo.

Jo whispered to the Doctor, 'Are they mad? Why are they calling us Dragons?'

'Some kind of an illusion,' replied the Doctor. 'Just

as you saw the older man as a Drashig for a few moments. Something very intriguing is going on.'

'You two,' Hardy shouted, 'shut up! You're our prisoners now.'

The strong voice spoke again over the loudspeaker. 'If you resist we can destroy you with our neutronic weapons.'

Stewart, some confidence returned now they had two Draconian prisoners, shouted into the microphone: 'If you destroy our ship you won't get the cargo.'

'So *that's* what it's all about,' murmured the Doctor. 'Piracy in Space.'

The voice spoke again, 'Open the hatch of your airlock.'

Stewart shouted back into the microphone. 'We have captured two of your soldiers. If you try to enter by force they'll be killed.'

Jo spoke up. 'What do you mean—soldiers? This is the Doctor and I'm——'

'Shut up!' roared Hardy.

Again the strong voice over the loudspeaker. 'We shall now enter your ship by force.'

Stewart turned to Hardy. 'You'd better lock them in the hold.'

Hardy poked the muzzle of his blaster gun into Jo's ribs. 'Get moving, back the way you came.'

'Do as he says,' said the Doctor quietly. 'The poor chap's in a very irrational state.'

As Hardy took the two prisoners back down the ship's corridor, Stewart re-tuned the transmitter to the Earth Control wavelength. 'Earth Chargo Ship C-982,' he spoke into the microphone. 'Draconian battle cruiser has now locked on. They are about to force entry. We are alone in Space. We need immediate help . . .'

But he had the feeling no help would arrive in time, and this would be the last message he'd ever send.

2

The Draconian Prince

Millions of miles from the threatened spaceship, the President of Earth was receiving the Draconian Ambassador in her spacious white office. She was an attractive woman in her forties, very feminine in her long pink robes, and her intelligent face suggested great inner strength. She was by no means the first female President of Earth. By her side was General Williams, a strikingly handsome man just a few years older than herself. He wore a single, metallic blue tunic with one simple star on his left breast to designate his rank. The Ambassador, dressed in black robes with high pointed shoulders, had the typical Draconian's dragon face, green scaly skin and tapering ears. He was a Prince of Draconia by birth and had both the dignity and arrogance that went with his station in life. The planet Draconia, despite technical advance equal to Earth's, had remained a monarchy with an Emperor, princes, and a Royal Court.

The President, who wished her visitor would sit down instead of towering over her, smiled up to the Ambassador Prince. 'I assure you, Your Highness, all these charges made against Earth are false. We are not attacking Draconian spaceships, nor have we ever done so.'

An Earth guard signalled to General Williams from the doorway, a circular opening in the brilliant white wall. Quietly the General crossed to the guard and took a folded note from him.

The Prince spoke in a clear, icy voice. 'Madam President, our soldiers have seen the Earthmen attack our ships. Our cargoes have been stolen. We Draconians do not tell lies.'

The President replied, 'The honour of your race is well known, Your Highness. We, the people of Earth, are indeed fortunate to share the galaxy of the Milky Way with such noble neighbours. That is why we cannot understand your actions.' In the best traditions of diplomacy, the President flavoured her criticisms with compliments.

'What actions?'

'You attack our spaceships. You steal our cargoes. You ignore our protests and meet them only with these counter-charges.'

It was impossible for the President to tell if the Prince was angry. Draconian green faces were incapable of turning red. Yet by the Prince's sudden movement, holding back his head so that the dragon snout protruded pugnaciously, he was clearly very annoyed. 'Our charges are true, Madam. Yours are false. We do not attack your ships——'

By now General Williams had read the note. He crossed to the President's desk, breaking all convention by cutting in when the Prince was speaking. 'Madam President, you should see this immediately.'

She read the note, her face setting hard. Then she looked up to the Prince. 'This is a transcript of a distress call from one of our ships, Your Highness. Allow me to read it to you. "From Earth Cargo Ship C-982. We are under attack by a Draconian battle cruiser, Galaxy class, equipped with neutronic missiles."'

The Prince was quick to answer. 'The treaty between our two inter-stellar empires established a frontier in Space. We have never violated that frontier to attack your ships. But you have invaded our half of the galaxy many times.'

General Williams could no longer contain himself. 'In pursuit of your ships when they had raided ours!'

'General Williams!' The President was angry. She needed the General, perhaps more than he realised, and accepted his abrupt manner as part of his personality. But when she was in conference with the official representative of the one great power in Space that could destroy Earth, she intended to keep the conversation cool and polite.

The General realised he had overstepped the mark. He turned to the Prince and inclined his head. 'I apologise, Your Highness, for my momentary rudeness.'

The Prince neither spoke nor looked at the General.

The President, to relieve the tension, asked General Williams if a rescue attempt had been set in train.

'Unfortunately,' replied the General, 'I cannot answer that, Madam President. This note has only just been handed to me.'

'Then I suggest you look into that matter right away,' she said.

The General realised he was being sent from the room. 'As you wish, Madam President.' He inclined his head again to the silent Draconian Prince and left the vast white room.

The Prince waited until General Williams was out of earshot. 'Your General is insolent, Madam. We know the hatred he has always felt for our people. Long ago he caused a war. Now he wishes to do so again.'

The President felt freer to speak her real thoughts without the General being present. 'He is a soldier, Your Highness, and he is angry. The people of Earth are angry.'

'So are the nobles of my father's Royal Court,' countered the Prince. 'Anger and indignation are not the exclusive prerogative of the Earthmen.'

She let that pass. 'I want you to take my personal appeal to your father the Emperor. He must order an end to these attacks. If Draconia has some grievance against Earth, this is not the way to deal with it.'

Again the Prince threw back his head, his snout jutting forward. 'Many of our noblemen felt it was a mistake to make a treaty with Earth! Perhaps they were right. You attack our ships. When we protest you try to trick us with lies and evasions. Madam, I give you a final warning. The path you are treading leads only to war. And in war Draconia will destroy you!'

Having issued his threat, the Prince bowed stiffly and mumbled the meaningless diplomatic farewell of the twenty-sixth century. 'May you live a long life and may energy shine on you from a million suns.'

The President rose and started to reply. 'And may water, oxygen and plutonium be found in abundance——' But the Prince had already turned his back on her and was walking out of the great room.

Slowly, thoughtfully, the President sat down. Though she had denied the Draconians' allegations, it was hard to believe that such a proud people would have fabricated these claims that Earthmen were attacking their spaceships. She started to think about General Williams and wondered how much he really knew. The mass of the Earth's people had elected her as President because she stood for peace and compromise. In the great political debate before the last presidential election, General Williams had made it known that he favoured an aggressive inter-stellar policy. After the election results were declared, the President was quick to invite General Williams to be her military aide, to heal political wounds and show there were no hard feelings. She also hoped that by having Williams working for her he would not set himself to work against her peace policy. Yet was he now secretly engineering these attacks on Draconian spaceships in order to bring Earth's people to a war-like frame of mind?

She wished she knew the answer. Without thinking she opened the old-fashioned silver locket that hung from her simple necklace. The tiny photograph of General Williams, then a mere lieutenant and only twenty years old, looked up at her. She wondered if he, too, remembered back to when they were both young.

Hardy repeatedly prodded the Doctor in the back with the snout of his blaster gun as they went down the spaceship corridor.

'You don't have to keep doing that,' complained the Doctor. 'We're going quietly.'

Hardy said, 'I only have to squeeze this trigger and you'll be a dead Dragon, so shut your snout.'

'My snout!' exclaimed the Doctor, aware that he was rather good looking. 'I don't have a snout——'

'Stop here,' Hardy ordered.

The trio stopped by a metal door. A grille with bars was set high in the door. 'Pull that open,' said Hardy. The Doctor gripped the grille and pulled the door towards him. It led into a very small compartment.

'Now get in there.'

The Doctor stepped aside for Jo to go in first. Jo turned to him. 'What is this?'

'Sometimes we carry live cargo,' said Hardy. 'Animals.'

'But we aren't animals,' Jo protested.

'You're Dragons,' said Hardy. 'What's the difference? The sooner your lot are exterminated, the better.' He slammed the door shut.

Immediately the Doctor began to rummage in a capacious pocket and pulled out his sonic screwdriver, aiming it at where he expected the lock to be. There was no lock. From outside they heard Hardy slide two old-fashioned bolts across the door. The Doctor shrugged and put away the sonic screwdriver. Neither of them spoke until they had heard Hardy's footsteps go back up the corridor.

'Doctor, why do they keep calling us Dragons?'

'Because that's how they see us, Jo.'

'But why Dragons?'

'Some non-human life form, something they're frightened of.' The Doctor had a flash of realisation. 'Of course—*Draconians*!'

'What?'

The Doctor was excited by his deduction. 'If this is the period I think it is, there are two great empires spreading through the galaxy of the Milky Way—Earth and Draconia, both expanding, colonising one planet after another, and coming into head-on collision.'

'The history lesson's very interesting,' Jo began, but the Doctor let her go no further.

'Not history, Jo, at least not *your* history. For you, coming from Earth in its twentieth century, this is the future.'

'Whatever it is,' she said patiently, 'why do they mistake us for these—what did you say?'

'Draconians. Dragons is a rather unflattering nickname the Earth people use. You remember that sound you heard?'

'Yes ...'

'And then we ran into that chap with the gun?'

Jo suddenly went white with fear and cowered away from the door. 'No, I don't want to remember!'

The Doctor gently touched her arm. 'Think, Jo. Concentrate. What did you see?'

'I saw ... I saw ...' She covered her face with her hands. 'I saw a Drashig!'

'No you didn't, Jo. You saw that man. But the sound made you see the thing you most fear.'

Jo slowly took her hands from her face. 'How?'

'Oh, it wouldn't be too difficult. Probably ultrasonics geared to stimulate the fear centres in the brain.'

Jo thought about this. 'It only lasted with me a short time, yet that man kept seeing us as Dragons—Draconians, that is.'

'Maybe it affects different people in different ways,' said the Doctor. 'What interests me is why someone has gone to all this trouble to make people see things that aren't really there.'

Jo nodded but she was busy looking at the small barred grille set in the door. 'Doctor, we've got to get out of here.' She stood on tiptoes and peeped out. 'I can just see the TARDIS.'

The Doctor smiled. 'Well, that's some consolation, but not much use while we're locked up in here.'

The Draconian voice repeated its warning over the ship's loudspeaker. 'If you surrender your cargo you will not be harmed.'

'I bet they always say that. They promise not to harm you, then they come on board and kill.' Stewart's mind was filled with thoughts of his comfortable two-roomed bachelor apartment on Earth, and of the girl-friend he had hoped to see after this trip. He was twenty-five and strongly believed he was too young to die. He desperately wished he could open his eyes, wake up and find this was all a nightmare.

'You're the one who said it would all blow over,' Hardy reminded his young companion.

'I meant there wouldn't be war,' said Stewart, not now with very much conviction. 'It's madness for the Draconians to carry on like this. They've got so much to lose, just as we have.'

'Maybe they *are* mad,' said Hardy. 'They look mad enough. I had half a mind to shoot those two prisoners instead of locking them away. Anyway, let's try again.' He spoke into the stalk microphone. 'Emergency, emergency. This is Earth Cargo Ship C-982 on co-ordinate 8972–6483——'

The Draconian voice came again over the loud-speaker. 'It's no use, Earthmen. We know your emergency wavelength and we are jamming it. No one on Earth will hear your cries for help now.'

Hardy pushed the microphone away. 'So that's that.'

Stewart could still feel his heart pounding. 'They must have heard our first message on Earth. They're probably already sending help, a battle cruiser with a commander who'll reason with them.'

Hardy shook his head. 'Listen, son, I'll tell you what they'll do on Earth. They'll send a polite note of protest round to the Draconian Embassy. That stupid President you voted for, she'll be inviting the Dragon Ambassador round for afternoon tea. I tell you, the Government should have blown the Dragons out of Space years ago.'

In his nervousness Stewart tried to joke. 'You're a real warmonger, Hardy.'

'What do you think this is? It's as bad as war.'

Stewart avoided Hardy's eyes. 'Look, the door of our spaceship is pure durilium. They're not going to get through that in a hurry.'

The Draconian voice broke in on his words. 'Earthmen, we are losing patience. This is your final warning. Surrender your cargo now or you will be destroyed.'

Stewart felt a terrible dryness in his mouth. He looked at the two blaster guns Hardy had laid on the floor. Slowly he reached down and picked one up. As he felt the heavy metal in his hands strength seemed to grow in him. At least he would die fighting. 'We'd better get down to the air lock,' he said quietly.

Hardy hadn't yet touched the second blaster gun. 'Going to be a hero for a cargo of flour?'

'I'm going to kill a Dragon before they kill us.' Stewart rose from his seat and walked down the corridor. After a few moments Hardy stood up, picked up the gun, and followed Stewart.

Alone in her white office, the President of Earth watched the news on television. At the touch of a button, the wall facing her instantly turned into a huge

24

television screen; the news-reader's face in close-up was twelve feet high, in perfect natural colour, with totally realistic depth.

'... and the Bureau of Population Control announced today that the recently reclaimed Arctic Areas are now ready for habitation ...'

As a democracy, Earth's news service was independent of government control. What was said on television affected the thinking, and therefore the votes, of hundreds of millions of Earth people. The President always watched the news two or three times each day, to find out what her voters would think of her peace policy.

The newscaster was starting now on another item. 'News is coming in of another Draconian attack on an Earth cargo ship. This is the third attack on Earth spaceships this month. As usual the Draconian Government, through its Embassy on Earth, denies all knowledge of the attack. Our President has not yet made any comment, but Congressman Brook, Leader of the Opposition, told one of our reporters——' The newscaster's face was replaced on the screen by that of Congressman Brook, the President's main opponent in the Earth Senate. He had a strong yet kindly face, auburn hair and twinkling eyes. He always spoke slowly and convincingly, as though each word had been carved in granite. Hundreds of millions of Earth people adored him.

'The people of Earth will no longer tolerate these unprovoked attacks,' he announced. 'It is time for Earth to take a stand and issue a final ultimatum to the Draconian Emperor. Since the days of St George, Earthmen have been perfectly capable of putting Dragons in their place——'

The President pressed the button again and the television screen vanished. She was disgusted by Brook's use of the word 'Dragons', a direct appeal to people's emotions. Because Brook had no power on Earth, he could say anything he pleased that might gain him votes. The President, however, had always to observe the diplomatic niceties.

She looked up to see General Williams enter by the round door. She burst out angrily, 'I ordered a complete security blackout on this present incident, yet here it is on television.'

Williams shrugged his powerful shoulders. 'The news services have their own Space radio monitors, Madam President. Probably they picked up the cargo ship's distress signals.'

She looked away from him. 'Or someone leaked the information.'

Williams knew what she meant by that insinuation. He preferred to ignore it. 'I came to tell you, Madam President, that a rescue ship should rendezvous with the cargo ship in seven minutes from now.'

'Good. Thank you.'

He continued. 'It'll be too late, of course. All they'll find will be dead men and an empty ship.'

'We can't be sure,' said the President. 'There have been survivors in other attacks.'

'Yes, one or two.' He paused for effect. 'I'm sure that's a great consolation to the people of Earth.'

'The people of Earth want peace, General Williams. That's why they made me President.'

'Moods change, Madam. You were elected before the Draconians started raiding our ships—and getting away with it.'

The President's hand strayed to touch the locket that contained his photograph, the one he didn't know she had. 'Are you now on the side of the Opposition, General Williams?'

He moved uneasily. 'I believe an ultimatum should go to the Draconian Emperor, Madam. All attacks must cease immediately and they should be made to pay for stolen cargoes.'

'I see. And what happens if they reject such an ulti-matum?'

'They wouldn't dare. Once they see we mean busi-ness they'll back down.'

The President had heard this argument many times before. It was a simple way of thinking that failed to consider all the consequences. 'But what if they don't back down? What if they continue to deny any know-ledge of these attacks? And before you answer, remem-ber that they claim our battle cruisers attack their cargo ships.'

He gave a short laugh. 'They have to say that. We know it's a ridiculous allegation. Our armed fleet is under strict orders not to interfere with any Draconian ships, except to defend our own.'

'All right,' said the President, 'let's presume that we are above reproach. I come back to my main question: if we issue an ultimatum and the Draconian Emperor rejects it, what am I supposed to do?'

He looked her straight in the eyes. 'Should that hap-pen, Madam President, there would be only one course open to us.' He stopped.

'Well? Tell me what it is.'

Now he could no longer hold her gaze. 'You know the answer, Madam President.'

'But I want you to say the word, General Williams.'

He straightened his shoulders defiantly. 'War.'

The President sat back in her chair. 'Exactly. You began your military career by starting a war with the Draconians. Are you so eager to begin another?'

The General's face was suffused with sudden anger. 'If you will excuse me, Madam President.' He turned smartly on his heel to go.

'Please, wait.' Her voice was soft. She could not af-ford to make an enemy of General Williams. 'I had no right to say that.'

The General turned back to face her, 'It was over

twenty years ago, Madam, yet you've forgotten nothing.'

'Have you?' she asked softly.

'I remember that you refused to see me or speak to me on the journey home.'

'Because you'd destroyed everything we had worked for,' she reminded him. 'We went to meet the Draconians and make peace. Once you opened fire on them, war was inevitable.'

'They were about to open fire on us,' the General protested. 'I did what had to be done—I struck first. If it's necessary, I shall do the same again.'

She shook her head. 'There will be no second war with the Draconians if I can prevent it.'

'But, Madam, don't you see, you're doing everything possible to start another war.'

The force of his words surprised her. 'I, start another war? What do you mean?'

'By giving way to them,' he pleaded. 'Don't you see, they're testing us with all these spasmodic attacks. They want to see if we have the nerve to fight back. Convince them that we will not tolerate their attacks and they'll treat us as equals!'

'And if not?'

'They will despise us,' said the General. 'They'll make Earth and its colonies a part of the Draconian Empire. We shall be their slaves.'

While the President and General Williams talked on Earth, in Space Hardy and Stewart prepared to do battle for their lives. They stood in the corridor of the spaceship, blaster guns aimed at the durilium air-lock door. A section of the door already glowed red hot as the boarding party on the other side applied thermal torches to burn their way in.

Hardy spoke laconically, 'So where's the battle cruiser that's going to rescue us?'

'We're a long way from Earth,' said Stewart. 'But they must be sending help.'

'Some hope.' As Hardy watched, more of the metal door began to glow red hot. 'The Dragons will be through any minute.'

In the cubicle further down the corridor, the Doctor had taken his sonic screwdriver to pieces and was adjusting its internal structure. Jo watched impatiently.

'What are you doing?'

The Doctor concentrated on his work for a full half minute, until he had the sonic screwdriver re-assembled. 'I've reversed the polarity of the screwdriver's power-source, converting it into an extremely powerful electro-magnet.'

'What's that going to do for us?'

'Wait and see, Jo. Wait and see.'

The Doctor had already put his hand through the grille in the door, groping to find the bolts that held them prisoner. His long slender fingertips could just touch both bolts, but he had failed to grip them. He put his hand through again, holding the screwdriver to the end of one bolt. As he manoeuvred the screwdriver, now a strong magnet, he and Jo could hear the bolt starting to slide in its bed.

Jo was excited. 'Can you open both of them?'

'With patience, Jo.' The Doctor continued to manoeuvre the screwdriver until he guessed the first bolt had been pulled clear. Then he re-positioned his arm and applied himself to sliding back the second bolt. This one moved quite easily. He withdrew his arm and pocketed the screwdriver. 'Perhaps this time, Jo, I'd better go first.' He opened the door and found himself looking straight into Hardy's blaster gun. 'Oh dear, how very embarrassing. Sorry about that, old chap.'

The Doctor tried to close the door again but Hardy put his foot in the way.

'Out,' ordered Hardy.

Jo asked, 'What for? I thought you wanted us in here.'

'We've changed our minds,' said the space pilot. 'We're going to meet your friends.'

'We keep ourselves very much to ourselves,' said the Doctor. 'We don't have any friends.'

'Any arguments and I kill one of you right here.' Hardy's finger tightened round the trigger. 'Out!'

The Doctor looked at Jo. 'Out,' he said.

Once more the Doctor and Jo were propelled along the corridor at gunpoint. They arrived to see Stewart aiming his blaster at the now completely red hot durilium door.

'I wish you'd listen to us,' shouted Jo. 'We aren't Dragons or whatever you call them. I'm human, the same as yourselves.'

'You're part of their boarding party,' snapped Stewart. 'You are going to stand in front of us and get killed first, by your own side!'

The Doctor tried to argue. 'My dear fellow, since they haven't boarded you yet, how can we be part of their boarding party? Try to be logical.'

Stewart looked confused by the Doctor's reasoning. Then he shook his head as though trying to clear it of difficult thoughts. 'They're coming to rescue you.'

'Look out!' screamed Hardy. 'They're coming through!'

The whole door was finally dissolving in a cloud of smoke. Two giant figures appeared through the jagged opening. Huge man-like creatures with bald ape heads, wearing belted metal tunics, both carried handguns.

Jo screamed, 'Ogrons!'

'Well, I'll be . . .' For the Doctor this was an entirely unexpected development. He had met the Ogrons more than once in his travels, great hulking brutes with minds little more advanced than Earth's early cave-men. As he recalled, Ogrons had neither the wit nor cunning to get up to any devilry of their own, though they had been used by the Daleks and other advanced Space species to do their dirty work.

Hardy shouted, 'Keep back, you Dragons, if you want to save your friends.'

The Doctor turned to him. 'They're not Dragons, they're——'

But Hardy wasn't listening. He was convinced he faced two Draconians. 'I mean it. I'll shoot!'

Realising this was no time to argue, the Doctor ducked under Hardy's gun and sent the space pilot cannoning into one of the Ogrons. The Ogron fired wildly, hitting Stewart at close range. The Doctor, meantime, had grabbed Jo's arm and was dragging her down the corridor back towards the TARDIS. One of the Ogrons felled Hardy with a single blow from its huge furry hand and lumbered after the fleeing couple.

The TARDIS in sight, the Doctor fumbled in his pocket for the key.

'Watch out!' yelled Jo. Coming up behind them was the pursuing Ogron.

The Ogron raised its hand gun and fired. The Doctor sprawled forwards on to the deck. Jo threw herself down beside him. 'Doctor! Doctor!'

The Doctor remained still. Slowly Jo looked up. The Ogron stood over her, its gun pointed at her head.

3

Stowaways

General Williams sat watching the President as she dictated a statement into her desk microphone. 'Although distress signals have been received from yet another of our cargo ships, until the arrival of the Earth rescue ship we must reserve judgment. Relations between ourselves and the Draconian Empire are admittedly tense, but this is all the more reason not to indulge in ill-informed speculation which can only worsen the situation.' She paused, then decided that her last words suitably ended the statement. For the benefit of the technician who, in another part of the presidential palace, was recording her words, she said, 'Please have copies of that sent to all news services throughout Earth.' She touched a button that turned off the microphone.

Williams said quietly, 'Do you think that will satisfy the world?'

'Why not? It was the truth.'

He did not relish what he had to report to her. 'Madam President, there have been anti-Draconian riots in Tokyo and Belgrade, and the Draconian Consulate in Helsinki has been burnt to the ground. In Los Angeles demonstrators burnt an effigy of you.'

'I see.' She considered. 'We must compensate the Draconian Government for the loss of their consulate.'

'Really, Madam President!' Williams felt his temper flaring again. 'What about them compensating us for——'

A light on the desk telephone began to flash. The President lifted the phone. 'Yes?' She listened, then quietly replaced the phone. 'That cargo ship, it's just been found drifting in Space.'

'Any sign of the Draconians?' Williams had heard it all before and knew what the answer would be.

She shook her head. 'The rescue ship arrived too late to catch them. The Earth ship isn't responding to any signals. Our people are about to board it now. We'll soon know what really happened.'

'Perhaps,' said General Williams. 'If there's anyone alive to tell the story.'

The flashing lights and high-pitched buzzing inside the Doctor's mind slowly subsided. He realised he was lying face down on a metal deck and that somewhere a girl's voice was calling to him.

'Doctor! Over here!'

It was Jo's voice. The Doctor tried to move his arms first. They felt heavy as lead weights. Slowly he drew up his legs.

'Here, Doctor! I'm locked in here!'

He looked round to the source of the calling. The bolted door to the cubicle swam into vision. A hand, Jo's hand, protruded through the little grille, waving to draw attention. By now the Doctor's twin hearts were starting to pump blood through his veins. He staggered to his feet, lurched across the deck towards the cubicle door, slid away the two bolts. The door opened and Jo came out.

'Doctor, are you all right? I thought they'd killed you.'

He shook his head. 'Some kind of neutronic stun-gun. But why didn't they kill me?' He shook his head again, to clear it. 'What happened?'

'An Ogron threw me back into this little cell place, then they took all the cargo. And, Doctor ...'

'Yes, Jo?'

'They took the TARDIS.'

The Doctor looked at the corner where the TARDIS had materialised. It was empty.

'We're stranded,' said Jo. 'What are we going to do?'

The Doctor forced himself to recover quickly from the shock of losing the TARDIS. 'We'd better see what's happened to those two fellows.'

'But they wanted to kill us,' Jo protested.

'Because they thought we were Draconians. They may see things differently now. Come on.' The Doctor walked up the corridor towards the air-lock.

They found the air-lock door repaired and Hardy and Stewart lying unconscious near by. 'Both stunned,' said the Doctor, 'just as I was. They'll be all right.'

Jo was studying the repaired door. 'Why did the Ogrons go to all this trouble?'

'If they hadn't fixed the door,' explained the Doctor, we'd have lost all the air in the ship when they cast off, and we'd all be dead.'

'But why should that bother them?'

'Maybe they've got kind hearts, Jo. There's good in everyone, you know.'

Jo pulled a face. 'You're making fun of me, Doctor. Ogrons don't have kind hearts, and they certainly haven't got the intelligence to do all this *and* mend that door. Do you know what's really going on?'

'I'm thinking about it, Jo——'

The Doctor stopped short as he heard a voice coming from the flight deck. 'Look after these two fellows, Jo. I'll go and see what that is.' He hurried along the corridor to the flight deck. The voice was coming over the loudspeaker.

'... Do you read me? I repeat, this is Earth Battle Cruiser to Earth Cargo Ship C-982. We are now approaching you. Do you read me?'

The Doctor pulled the stalk microphone towards his lips. 'Hello, Battle Cruiser. This is the cargo ship.'

'What is your situation?'

'The ship has been attacked and the cargo stolen,'

34

replied the Doctor. 'The crew are stunned but other-wise unharmed.'

'We shall lock on five seconds from now,' said the voice. 'Stand by.'

The Doctor went back to Jo, who was giving a drink from a water pack to the semi-recovered Stewart. Even as the Doctor approached they heard the clang of the Earth battle cruiser locking on. The sound and the vibration startled Jo.

'It's all right,' said the Doctor. 'We're being rescued.'

Stewart looked up at Jo and the Doctor. 'Who are you people? What happened?'

The Doctor smiled. 'Don't worry, old chap. You're all right now, in safe hands.'

The air-lock door started to creak open. Stewart looked at it in sudden fear.

'The Dragons! They're boarding!'

'That's all in the past,' said the Doctor. 'The people coming on board now are friends.'

The air-lock door was now fully opened. The Captain of the Earth battle cruiser stepped forward warily, blaster gun at the ready. He was a short, stocky man, with a tough square chin. He wore trousers and tunic of metallic yellow with insignia to denote his rank. On seeing the Doctor—the velvet jacket and the frilly shirt—he registered restrained surprise. 'Who are you?' The Captain held his blaster gun aimed at the Doctor.

'We're passengers,' explained the Doctor.

'I see,' said the Captain, not seeing at all. 'Having a fancy dress party?' It wasn't a question that needed answering. He looked down at Stewart and Hardy on the deck. 'Is this all the crew?'

Stewart nodded. 'Me and my co-pilot. Dragons attacked us.'

'I'm Captain Gardiner,' said the newcomer, gun still at the ready. 'Did they get the cargo?'

'Everything,' said Jo.

35

'Including some rather valuable property of mine,' added the Doctor.

Captain Gardiner holstered his gun at last. 'Tough luck.' He moved to where Hardy was lying still unconscious and shook him roughly. 'Are you dead or just stunned?'

Hardy started to revive. 'Dragons ... They attacked us.'

'All right, we know.' Captain Gardiner straightened up. 'Passengers, you say? On a cargo ship? That's very unusual.' He looked back to Stewart, the more conscious of the two pilots. 'Where did you pick these two up?'

'Don't know,' said a dazed Stewart. 'Can't remember.'

Gardiner's voice became gruff. 'Pull yourself together, man! How did these two people get on board your ship?'

Stewart made a visible effort to concentrate. The one thing he couldn't sort out was the presence of this tall man and the young woman dressed in strange clothes. Carrying passengers on cargo ships was strictly forbidden. For his own sake he had to produce some explanation. 'Stowaways,' he said suddenly. 'That's right, they were stowaways!'

Hardy had regained his senses enough to realise the position he and Stewart were in. Even if stowaways had got themselves on board unnoticed by the crew, it could still result in a bad report on the pilots for lack of security. 'Not ordinary stowaways,' he said. 'They were helping the Dragons!'

Gardiner, who during his career as a military officer had heard every excuse, asked simply, 'How?'

Hardy flashed a glance to Stewart, hoping the younger man could think of a reason. Stewart said, 'They were ... they were sending signals, leading the Dragons to us.'

'That's right,' supported Hardy, pleased with Stew-

36

art's quick thinking. 'They were signalling to the Dragons to attack us.'

Jo exploded, 'That's absolute nonsense! We didn't want to be on this ship at all. It was an accident.'

Gardiner turned to her. 'Your companion said you were passengers. Passengers don't get on ships by accident.'

The Doctor produced his most winning smile. 'I merely wanted to avoid a lot of tiresome explanations, old chap. In any event, these two poor fellows are very confused. The people who attacked this ship weren't Draconians at all.'

To this Hardy retorted with all the force of a man who having told a lie was now in the enviable position of being able to tell the truth—or what he believed was the truth. 'He's trying to fool you, sir. They were Dragons all right. We saw them with our own eyes.'

Gardiner looked at the Doctor. 'Well?'

'These men's minds were attacked by some sort of hallucinatory device,' explained the Doctor. 'They're still suffering from the after-effects, trying to fit us into the pattern of their delusions.'

'I see,' said Captain Gardiner, not believing a word of it. 'And where *do* you fit?'

The Doctor ignored the question. 'It was some kind of ultra-sonic sound wave,' he went on. 'They thought they were seeing Draconians when in fact the ship was attacked by a completely different life form.'

'Ogrons,' said Jo, presuming the Captain would instantly understand what that meant.

The Doctor scowled at her. 'I wouldn't try to explain everything, not all at once.'

Captain Gardiner said dismissively, 'Either you are both raving mad or extremely dangerous.' He looked down at the two pilots again. 'Get up.'

Hardy and Stewart struggled to their feet, sheepishly avoiding the Doctor's eyes.

'I'll put two men on board to take this ship back to

Earth,' said Captain Gardiner. He turned to one of his soldiers who crowded behind him now in the air-lock. 'These two "stowaways", lock them in the hold and put a guard on them.'

Soldiers sprang forward to seize the Doctor and Jo.

Jo protested, 'But we haven't done anything!'

'You can explain that to Earth Security,' said Captain Gardiner crisply. 'But I don't expect they'll believe a word of it.'

The Doctor and Jo sat on upturned crates in the cubicle where they had been imprisoned before. Jo got up and looked through the door grille. 'There's a soldier watching the door.'

The Doctor remained where he was. 'That's what he's there for.'

She turned to him, urgency in her voice. 'Right. We'll give it a few minutes, then I'll start groaning and saying I'm ill, and when he comes in you can use your Venusian Karate.'

'Then what?'

She continued, full of enthusiasm. 'Well, we can take his gun and go to the flight deck and hi-jack the spaceship and force them to take us to Earth.'

'Jo, this ship *is* going to Earth.'

'That's a point.' She considered. 'Well what are we going to do, then?'

'Why don't you stop bobbing about, sit down and let me think?'

Crushed, Jo returned to her upturned crate and sat down. For a full half minute she was silent, as the Doctor had requested. Then, 'Doctor?'

'Mm?'

'Now that it's all over and the Ogrons have gone, why don't those crewmen remember what *really* happened?'

'They've constructed a new kind of reality,' explained the Doctor. 'The true facts have been erased from their minds.'

'But they're telling lies about us.'

'Partly lies, Jo, and partly what they believe to be the truth. They're desperately trying to fit us into *their* version of things. It must have been very strange for them when we suddenly appeared.'

'But we didn't,' she said. 'Two Draconians appeared —at least, that's what they thought.'

'When we get to Earth,' said the Doctor, 'we have to reach someone in authority, someone whose mind isn't closed.'

'Closed to what?'

'These people believe Draconians are attacking their spaceships, but we know it's Ogrons. We also know that Ogron's haven't the intelligence to set up this hallucinatory device that fools everyone.'

'And after that,' said Jo, 'all we have to do is to find the TARDIS and then we can go home. You make it sound very simple.' She sighed and settled down to wait.

The President and General Williams looked at the face of an Earth guard on the President's desk videophone.

'I am speaking from the cargo ship,' said the guard, a lieutenant called Kemp. 'Captain Gardiner is at the controls now. We shall land on Earth in fifteen minutes. The crew are safe. Also on board are two human stowaways of unknown origin.'

General Williams spoke towards the videophone. His voice would be heard by Lieutenant Kemp, ten thousand miles away in Space. 'I want a cordon round the landing area the minute that ship touches down. Nobody on, nobody off, till I get there. Understood?'

'Yes, sir.'

The President flicked a switch. The desk videophone went blank. 'You'll handle the interrogations yourself?'

'Of course,' said the General. 'I'll go there straight away.' His personal air-transporter was waiting in the palace grounds.

'Whatever you find, General, you'll report directly to me?'

About to leave, the General paused. 'Do you doubt my loyalty, Madam President?'

'No,' she said, with meaning. 'But I suspect Congressman Brook would dearly love to appear on world television with the two pilots from that cargo ship. He's done it before.'

Williams squared his shoulders. 'I shall report directly to you, Madam, and only to you.' He inclined his head. 'May you live a long life and may energy shine on you from a million suns,' he intoned stuffily.

The President smiled. She realised he was offended by having his loyalty questioned. 'And may water, oxygen and plutonium be found in abundance wherever you land,' she replied.

The General nodded and hurried from the white office.

Jo peered again through the little grille in the bolted door. The landing on Earth had been smooth, hardly a bump as the great cargo ship settled on its landing pad.

'What do you think they're doing?' she asked the Doctor. 'We've been landed for ages.'

'Twelve minutes to be exact, Jo. Just be patient.'

They waited in silence. From somewhere, probably the flight deck, they could hear a mumble of voices.

'They've no right to keep us locked up like this,' Jo said after a while. 'We've done nothing but try to be helpful.'

'Perhaps we'll have a chance to explain that ...' The

Doctor paused. Footsteps were coming along the corridor.

The bolts were pulled back, the door opened. A young Earth lieutenant stood in the doorway.

'You two,' said Lieutenant Kemp. 'On your feet and outside.'

Jo asked, 'Are we going to see someone in authority?'

'Indeed you are,' said Kemp. 'Now get moving.'

Earth soldiers with drawn blaster guns waited in the corridor. As the Doctor and Jo were taken to the flight deck, the soldiers kept their guns trained on the prisoners.

'Just one small question,' the Doctor turned to Lieutenant Kemp as they made their way forward, 'do you see me as a human or as a Draconian?'

Kemp replied, 'Shut up!'

The Doctor smiled. 'There's nothing like a friendly discussion.' He remained quiet until they reached the flight deck.

A transparent-topped table had been quickly erected and General Williams sat behind it. Flanking him were the two pilots, Hardy and Stewart, plus Captain Gardiner. As Lieutenant Kemp brought the prisoners in, he stood to attention and saluted General Williams. 'The stowaways, sir.' He turned to the Doctor and Jo. 'You stand there.' He indicated a place directly in front of the General.

'Certainly, old man,' said the Doctor genially. He addressed General Williams. 'How very nice to meet you, sir. If you and I could just have a little chat——'

Kemp shouted, 'Quiet! You are here to answer questions.'

The Doctor pretended to be apologetic. 'Terribly sorry, old man. What is it you all want to know?'

The General spoke. 'This is a special commission of inquiry under the Earth Security Order of the year

41

2539.' He turned to Kemp. 'Inform the prisoners of their legal rights.'

Lieutenant Kemp cleared his throat. He spoke rapidly and precisely. 'Under the Earth Security Order it is the duty of every Earth citizen to answer all questions fully and honestly. There shall be no legal representation, and all decisions of the Court shall be final and binding, against which there is no appeal.'

Jo protested, 'That means we've got no rights at all!'

The Doctor tried a gentler approach. 'Why don't we drop all these formalities, sir, and get on with the questions? We're perfectly willing to talk to you.'

General Williams concealed a smile at the Doctor's cheek. 'Tell me, for what purpose did you board this cargo ship?'

'For no purpose at all,' replied the Doctor honestly.

'Kindly answer my question,' said the General.

'It was an accident,' said Jo. 'We didn't want to come on board at all.'

The Doctor took up her argument. 'My spaceship and this one narrowly avoided a collision in hyperspace and somehow my ship materialised in the hold of your cargo ship.'

The General's eyes narrowed. 'What do you mean—materialised?'

'It's a thing the TARDIS can do,' Jo began. 'It can materialise ...' Her voice trailed off as she realised everyone was staring at her incredulously. '... just as it can de-materialise. Doctor, you'd better explain about that.'

'I need no explanation,' said the General. 'This is scientifically impossible.'

The Doctor was indignant. 'That, sir, depends on your kind of science! Earth science, even in this century, is very limited.'

'Anyway,' said Jo, 'that's what happened.'

'I see.' Clearly the General didn't see at all. 'And where is this so-called spaceship of yours now?'

42

'The Ogrons took it,' said Jo. 'When they stole your flour.'

'Ogrons?' queried the General.

Captain Gardiner touched a document on the table. 'It's in my report, sir. Whatever nonsense the prisoners told me, I carefully recorded it.'

'Yes, of course.' The General had only glanced at the report since his arrival from the presidential palace. 'So these creatures just picked up your spaceship and walked off with it?'

The Doctor nodded. 'It's a very small spaceship,' he explained.

By now the General was convinced he was faced with two lunatics or very cunning enemy agents. 'According to the crew you sent signals to guide the Draconians, then aided them to board and plunder this ship.'

'That's quite untrue,' the Doctor protested. 'The testimony of these two pilots is totally unreliable. 'They're suffering from deliberately induced hallucinations. They've simply incorporated us into the pattern of their delusion.'

'You must listen to us,' Jo pleaded. 'There was this strange sound. It makes you see things, the things you fear most. I even saw a Drashig!'

'A what?' asked the General, more convinced than ever that these people were mentally deranged.

'What my young friend is trying to say,' said the Doctor, 'is that this sound was transmitted from the Ogrons' spaceship. It made your two pilots see us as Draconians, and when the Ogrons boarded they saw them as Draconians, too.'

Jo turned to Hardy and Stewart. 'You thought *we* were Draconians first of all—remember? Now you say we're human stowaways. Try to remember what really happened.'

The General turned to the pilots. Both men looked disturbed and angry at Jo's insinuations. 'Well?'

'They're lying,' said Stewart. 'We know what we saw.'

'You saw what you expected to see,' said the Doctor. 'Do you remember the sound?'

For a moment Hardy and Stewart glanced at each other, and the Doctor had the impression that true memory was dawning in both of them. Then they avoided each other's eyes.

'We were attacked by the Dragons,' Hardy insisted. 'You were helping them!'

'Then what about the air-lock door?' asked the Doctor. 'It was re-sealed after the attack. Wasn't that odd?' He turned back to the General. 'The Ogrons wanted these two men to remain alive, to make sure the Draconians were blamed for the attack.'

General Williams smiled. 'You put forward convincing arguments, whoever you are. But these arguments are based on fallacies. A spaceship that can materialise inside another, that can be picked up and carried away, and now talk of Ogrons ... No, sir, this tribunal only deals in known facts. I suggest that the Draconians re-sealed the air-lock door to preserve the lives of their own two agents.'

'If you're going to adopt that attitude,' said the Doctor, 'there's little point continuing this discussion. I'd better talk to your superiors.'

General Williams said, 'Only the President is superior to this tribunal.'

'Very well,' said the Doctor. 'Let me talk to him.'

This brought quizzical looks from the Earthmen. 'Him?' said General Williams. 'Your masters didn't brief you very well. I'd have thought the Draconian Secret Service was reasonably aware that the President of Earth is a woman.'

'Then maybe she'll have sense enough to listen to us,' said Jo. 'When can we see her?'

'You won't,' replied the General curtly. 'You'll be taken to Security Headquarters for questioning. If you

44

are Draconian agents, they'll find out soon enough. The tribunal is closed.'

Jo shouted, 'But this isn't fair! You've taken no notice of us. You're so unreasonable!'

The Doctor and Jo were seized by Earth guards.

As the General stood up he turned to Jo for a parting word. 'Young woman, once you've been inside Security Headquarters you will think of me as the most reasonable man you've ever met.'

4

The Mind Probe

Half an hour later General Williams found himself defending his actions to the President.

'Draconian agents? Are you sure, General Williams?'

'What else can they be, Madam President? Their story is obviously nonsense.'

'But why did the Draconians leave them on the cargo ship after the attack?'

'Perhaps they hoped we would accept them as simple stowaways,' said the General. He had not given much thought to these possibilities. 'The punishment for stowaways can be as little as a hefty fine. They thought these two would soon be loose within Earth society to spy for them.' He knew there were many holes in this argument, so quickly went on to the central issue. 'The fact we must face, Madam President, is that the Draconian Empire is preparing for war——'

She raised her hand. 'So you presume, General. There is still no proof.'

'The continued attacks on our cargo ships are no way of establishing friendly relations, Madam.'

She knew there was no answer to that. 'If you are right in believing these two humans to be Draconian agents, the sooner we confront the Draconians with their duplicity the better.' She had a sudden thought. 'Have the prisoners brought here.'

'To your palace, madam?' The General was amazed.

'I want to see them, and I intend to bring them face to face with His Highness, the Draconian Ambassador.'

*

The Doctor and Jo were taken from the cargo space-ship in what Captain Gardiner referred to as a ground-transporter. This was an ultra-streamlined coach with seating for up to thirty passengers. It had barred windows and a heavily locked door, and the word *Security* painted along both sides of its black body. It did not, however, have any wheels. When the driver touched the starter control, the coach lifted a few inches off the ground and glided forward. The driver and the four guards who arrived with the coach wore distinctive black tunics and helmets also bearing the word *Security*. They were all armed with blaster guns; batons, handcuffs and personal radios hung from their heavy black belts. They treated Captain Gardiner with the same indifference afforded to the Doctor and Jo.

The coach sped fast through almost deserted city streets. Occasionally they caught glimpses of crowds of people in metallic coloured tunics on escalators, or in piazzas between the high buildings, and sometimes vehicles flashed by in the opposite direction, huge buses packed with people, but there were no small individually driven cars, as Jo was used to in her time in history. Most of the buildings were identical in design and colour, and so tall it was impossible to see the sky from the Security coach.

The driver turned into a narrow street that ended in high gates, which slid open as it approached. The coach went through, the gates shut behind it, then stopped in a square, concrete courtyard.

One of the guards positioned himself by the coach door. 'Out!' she shouted. The Doctor and Jo shuffled forward, down the step on to the concrete. 'Forward march!'

Flanked by guards, the Doctor and Jo marched towards a plain metal door set in the windowless wall. They passed through into a wide, low-ceiling corridor, and the door slid shut behind them. At the end of the

47

corridor was another metal door. Inside a black-uniformed man sat at a desk.

'What punishment?' he asked as the party entered.

Captain Gardiner stepped forward. 'These people haven't been convicted. General Williams just wanted you to hold them,' he paused, 'and to interrogate them.'

The man behind the desk gave the shadow of a grin. 'With pleasure. Who are you?'

Gardiner produced his credentials, a plastic card carrying his photograph and identity number.

'That's in order, Captain Gardiner.' The Security officer handed back the plastic card. 'Right, first we starve them a little, then we interrogate. Take them to cell 302.'

'About turn!' shouted one of the guards.

The Doctor and Jo were marched out, back down the corridor, through another metal sliding door, to a row of cell doors. A guard kicked the Doctor in the back as he entered the cell. The door slid shut.

Jo looked round the cell. It had two concrete bunks, nothing else. 'There's no place like home.'

'It could be worse, Jo.'

'It could be my own bedroom with clean white sheets and a stereo in the corner and colour television and a hot bath, if your rotten TARDIS didn't keep going off course!'

To her surprise the door opened. Captain Gardiner entered and looked round the sparse cell. 'I didn't think it would be as bad as this.'

Jo said, 'Come to taunt?'

'Not exactly.' The Captain lowered his voice. Guards stood outside the open door. 'I didn't like this business about starving you. When did you last eat?'

'A thousand years ago,' said Jo.

'My young friend means we haven't eaten for some time,' the Doctor quickly put in. 'But there's something more important than that. I've got to get a mes-

48

sage to your President.'

The Captain shook his head. 'Not a chance.'

Jo walked up to him. 'Why don't you listen to reason for a change? Hasn't it occurred to you that we may be telling the truth?'

Gardiner looked uneasy. 'I don't want to get mixed up with Security. It isn't healthy. But I might get them to feed you.'

The Doctor grinned. 'That's jolly decent of you, old chap.'

'I'll do what I can.' Captain Gardiner backed to the door. 'But let me give you some good advice. You're going to tell them everything sooner or later. They'll use the mind probe, I think they always do when treachery is suspected. So make it easy for yourselves, tell them everything before they set to work. Meantime I'll try and get you some food.' He went back through the door and a guard closed it.

Jo turned to the Doctor. 'I didn't like the sound of that. What did he mean—mind probe?'

The atmosphere in the President's office was tense. Standing before her was the Draconian Ambassador. To one side stood the space pilots Hardy and Stewart, dressed now in smart grey uniform tunics, to the other side General Williams. The President could feel the hatred emanating from the two pilots towards the Ambassador.

'You're quite sure it was a Draconian battle cruiser?' she asked Hardy, addressing him as the older of the two men.

'No doubt about it, Madam. They locked on and boarded us. We both saw them. They were Dragons——' Hardy corrected himself. 'I mean, they were Draconians all right.'

'Thank you,' said the President. 'You can go now. I hope you will soon be fully recovered from your ordeal.' She nodded to General Williams who ushered the two pilots to the door. Then she turned to the Ambassador. 'Well, Your Highness?'

'With all respect that is due to you, Madam President,' said the Draconian, his voice cold and words clipped, 'those men are your servants.' He stole a glance at Williams, now returning to the desk. 'They say what they have been ordered to say.'

'Ordered by whom?'

The Ambassador spoke as though from a prepared speech. 'It is not the policy of the Emperor's Government to interfere in the internal politics of a neighbouring empire, but clearly there are those among you who seek hostility with us.'

Williams, who realised all this was directed against himself, spoke up. 'On this occasion, Your Highness, we have more than our servants to confront you with. We captured two of your human agents.'

A deep hiss of anger came from the Ambassador's green snout. 'We have no human agents! Subversion and espionage is expressly forbidden by the Treaty of Peace between our two empires.'

'A treaty which you have broken,' remarked the General.

The Ambassador gathered his cloak. 'With your permission, Madam President, I shall return to my embassy——'

She rose, a restraining hand outstretched. 'No, please, Your Highness. I'm sure the General regrets his rudeness. But I would like you to see these two human prisoners.' She nodded to the General. He was already half way to the opening in the wall, where guards were bringing in the Doctor and Jo. 'General Williams, please explain to His Highness who these people are.'

The Doctor and Jo, flanked by palace guards, were brought forward to the President's desk.

'These people,' said the General, 'stowed away on

the cargo ship that your battle cruiser attacked, Your Highness. They transmitted signals which enabled your people to home-in on their prey.'

The Ambassador stared at the two prisoners. 'I know nothing of these humans.'

'Perhaps *you* don't,' said the President. 'But someone in the Draconian Empire employed them.'

Jo blurted out, 'This is all stupid! You've all got it wrong!'

'If someone would have the courtesy to listen to me,' said the Doctor, 'perhaps I might explain that we are not employed by anyone.'

The Ambassador turned from the prisoners to face the President. 'How can these two humans, found on an Earth spaceship, concern the Draconian Empire?'

'Because you put them there!' General Williams face reddened with anger at what he thought was the Ambassador's evasion. 'They are traitors to their own race, bribed by you!'

'We aren't bribed by anyone,' insisted the Doctor. 'We are harmless civilian travellers, being very badly treated——'

'Quiet!' stormed the General. 'You were part of the Draconian attack on our cargo ship.'

'There was no Draconian attack,' answered the Doctor. 'The attack was made by Ogrons.'

The President looked to General Williams. No one had explained this to her. 'What are they talking about, General?'

He scoffed. 'They've invented some ridiculous story about a totally unknown life-form. It's obviously an attempt to protect their Draconian masters.'

The Doctor asked patiently, 'If we were working for the Draconians, why did they leave us on your ship after the attack?'

'To act as spies,' replied the General, 'when you were brought back to Earth.'

'Allow me to congratulate you, sir. You have the

most totally closed mind I have ever met.'

'You'll regret your insolence.' The General turned to the palace guards. 'Take them away. Security Headquarters have my personal permission to use any means to extract the truth from them!'

The guards closed in on the Doctor and Jo.

'Madam President,' pleaded the Doctor, 'I beg you to listen to me. Some third party is trying to provoke war between Earth and Draconia. You're both being duped.'

'I said take them away,' the General commanded.

The guard twisted the prisoners' arms behind their backs, yanked them round to propel them out of the room.

'One moment,' said the President calmly. She looked to the Doctor who had turned his head round to see her. 'Why should a third party, as you claim, wish to do this?'

'I've no idea, Madam, but I believe that is what's happening.'

The General stepped forward, blocking the Doctor's view of the President. 'Madam President, may I suggest that you leave these prisoners to me?'

The Doctor did not see or hear the President's reply. At a nod from the General, the palace guards increased their grip on the Doctor's twisted arms and pushed him forward out of the room. He called back, 'Your two empires are going to be plunged into the most terrible war if you don't listen. For heaven's sake show some sense ...' But by now he and Jo were outside the office. Black uniformed Security guards were waiting for them.

With the prisoners gone, the Ambassador turned to the President. 'Is that the evidence upon which you accuse me?'

The President sat down at her desk. For some moments she was lost in thought. Then, solemnly, she spoke. 'Your Highness, I must ask you to convey a formal protest to your Emperor.'

The Draconian bristled. 'I shall certainly report to him this latest insult to the honour of the Draconian Empire!' He stood to his full height. 'May you live a long life and may energy shine on you from a million suns.' Without waiting for the formal reply, he turned and left the room.

For a few moments neither the President nor the General spoke. She broke the silence. 'We have greatly offended him, you know.'

'Possibly.' The General was not one to mind causing offence. 'We should have used the mind probe *before* showing these prisoners to the Ambassador. We should have confronted him with a full confession.'

'Does it occur to you that they may be telling the truth?'

He looked quizzically at her. 'Are you serious?'

She nodded. 'I'm putting the possibility to you.'

'A possibility we should discount,' he said emphatically. 'Can you seriously believe in a life-form that can change its appearance and look like something else—in a pocket spaceship that materialises inside another?'

'I suppose you're right,' she replied slowly. 'The whole thing is rather nonsensical. But who *are* these two people?'

'Leave me to find that out,' answered the General, preparing to go. 'I'll get the truth out of them. They'll regret the day they tried lying to us!'

5

Kidnap

The Draconian Embassy was one of the few houses in the city to stand in its own quiet gardens. From the Ambassador's main office he could look out on a small lawn, a few stunted trees and carefully tended flowers. Though the house was typical of Earth design, with straight walls and windows, the interior had been decorated in Draconian style. Clever interior designers had re-fashioned some of the walls to make them curve in the way Draconian eyes found pleasant. The predominant colour of the paintwork and also the curved, rounded furniture was green.

The Ambassador and his First Secretary, an older Draconian with many years experience in the Draconian Diplomatic Service, stood as they talked. 'I ask myself,' said the Ambassador, 'why should the Earthmen produce such an elaborate lie?'

The First Secretary nodded his green head, a form of politeness when talking to a social superior. 'Their ways are devious, Your Highness. They are an inscrutable species.'

'Obviously they are preparing the second stage of their plan. First the attacks on our cargo ships, and now this.'

The First Secretary nodded again. 'Is it possible, Your Highness, that for once the Earthmen spoke the truth? Some plan of your father the Emperor, of which even Your Highness has not been informed?'

The Ambassador's right nostril twitched, a sign of disagreement. 'The Emperor would not contemplate such a plan. We do not break the Treaty of Peace.'

The First Secretary realised he had said the wrong

thing. He quickly changed the subject. 'Shall I prepare Your Higness's report to the Emperor on your meeting with the Earth President?'

The Ambassador considered. 'I must have more information.'

'Would it not be useful to interrogate the humans who were found on the Earth cargo ship?'

'You do not understand,' replied the Ambassador. 'They are prisoners, accused of treachery to their planet.'

'Agreed,' said the First Secretary. 'But prisoners have been known to escape.'

The Ambassador studied the First Secretary's snout. 'I could not countenance such a plan. It would be undiplomatic.'

'Of course, Your Highness. But should two escaping prisoners seek sanctuary in this embassy it would be less than Draconian to turn them away.'

The Ambassador slowly turned his back on the First Secretary. 'I must not detain you longer. No doubt you have important duties demanding your attention.'

The First Secretary, understanding exactly the meaning of this last remark, bowed to the Ambassador's back, turned and left the room. He had an important telephone call to make.

A girl telephonist spoke to the President on her desk videophone. 'The First Secretary of the Draconian Embassy wishes to speak to you, Madam President.'

'Put him through.'

The green dragon face of the First Secretary appeared on the screen. 'I am honoured that you consent to speak to me, Madam President.'

The President answered, 'It is always my pleasure to be in communication with representatives of your Emperor. How may I be of service to you?'

'His Highness the Ambassador wishes to speak again

to the two Earth people found on the cargo ship—in your presence of course, Madam President.'

The request surprised her. 'May I ask why?'

'His Highness feels that such an interrogation would convince you'—He paused slightly, to underline his next words—'you and your closest advisers that they are not agents of Draconia.'

The request seemed reasonable. Anything which might improve relations between the two empires appealed to the President. 'I shall have them brought here immediately. I suggest that His Highness joins me. We will question them together.'

'The President is most kind,' said the Draconian First Secretary. 'May you live a long life and may energy shine ...'

The Doctor and Jo were marched down another long concrete corridor inside the vast Security Headquarters prison.

Jo turned to one of the guards, 'You're sure it's the President who wants to see us again?'

The guard nodded. 'Instructions to take you to the presidential palace right away.' This summons seemed to impress the guards and they no longer shouted at the prisoners.

'Perhaps,' said the Doctor, 'she took heed of my good advice. Anyway, we shall soon see.'

The party approached one of the metal sliding doors. It slid upwards, revealing a walkway in a garden.

'*This* is part of the prison?' asked the Doctor.

A guard answered. 'It leads directly to the palace. A short cut. Come on.'

They moved forward. Jo was relieved to be in the open air again. She looked up at the trees and the cloudless blue sky. To her astonishment she saw a Draconian perched on a high wall, aiming a rifle at the party. At that instant the Draconian fired. The Security guard next to her fell backwards, sprawling on the concrete walkway. Before anyone could react, another Draconian fired his weapon, and a second Earth guard fell to the ground. The remaining two Security guards, who had now seen the Draconian snipers, tried to grab the Doctor and Jo. But the Doctor already had Jo by the arm and was rushing her towards a small cluster of trees. Realising their danger, the Security guards ran for cover. Alarm bells started clanging from the main prison building. As the fleeing prisoners approached the trees, other Draconians emerged suddenly from hiding, and rushed up to the prisoners to drag them away. The Doctor knocked down the first Draconian with a glancing blow, but three others moved forward to capture him.

'Jo,' he cried out, 'run for it. Get help!'

Jo ran in a frenzy across the lawn. Looking back for a moment she saw a Draconian fire a hand-gun point blank at the Doctor. He fell, stunned and was picked up by the Draconians and carried into the trees.

'We must demand the immediate withdrawal of the Draconian Embassy!' General Williams's face was flushed with anger. As he stood before the President's desk he seemed to quiver in rage.

'Break all diplomatic relations?' said the President. 'We don't know that the Ambassador was behind this abduction.'

'He is responsible for what his staff does, Madam President. The First Secretary deliberately tricked you.'

The President remained calm. 'Have the girl brought in, please.'

'What about their Embassy? The people of Earth will run riot when they hear of this insult.'

'In that case,' she said, 'they must not be told. It is your responsibility, General Williams, to ensure a

57

complete blackout of the incident.' She knew he could not disobey a presidential order. 'Please bring in the girl.'

With difficulty the General controlled himself. He went to the round doorway and nodded for Jo to be brought forward. She was accompanied by two palace guards, whom the President dismissed.

'Young woman,' began the President, 'the escape of your colleague puts you in a very serious position.'

'But it wasn't an escape,' said Jo. 'The Doctor was kidnapped.'

'Speak when you are spoken to,' barked the General. 'He was rescued by your Draconian paymasters.'

The President continued. 'Your wisest course is to make a full confession. Remember, your accomplice has left you to your fate.'

'But I haven't got anything *to* confess, Jo insisted. 'You've got it all wrong. The Doctor wanted to come here and talk to you. He was taken away by force.'

The General shook Jo by the shoulder. 'Your lies won't help you! When were you recruited? How many other agents do they have on Earth? What are their plans?' His temper mounting, he spun Jo round and glared into her face. 'Tell us voluntarily or under the mind probe—it makes no difference, except to you!'

'If you tell us everything,' said the President, 'I shall ensure that you are treated leniently.'

'But I don't know what you are talking about,' Jo cried out. 'We're not working for any Draconians. Don't you realise someone's trying to cause a war between you and the Draconians, and you're falling for it?'

General Williams released Jo's shoulders, as though in despair. 'We're wasting time. I propose depth interrogation with no further delay.'

Jo burst into tears. 'I don't care if you use your

stupid mind probe. I'm telling you the truth, and so was the Doctor.'

The President regarded Jo as tears cascaded down her cheeks. Then she spoke firmly, but with a touch of kindness. 'You're very young, my dear, and no doubt you've been led astray. But unless you tell us the whole truth immediately I shall be forced to let General Williams deal with the matter. The lives of millions of citizens may be at stake, and they are my only consideration. So you have the choice. Help us now by confessing everything. Or, if you prefer that the truth be wrung from you, afterwards you will be imprisoned for the rest of your life as a traitor to your planet.'

The Doctor's mind flashed on for less than a second. The optic nerve registered the picture of a green snout and pale green eyes looking down at him. Then blackness returned; he felt he was swimming in a sea of thick, dark oil.

A voice said, 'The Earthman is recovering. Come and look.' Feet moved on a highly polished floor. Voices mumbled. The blackness gave way to light. Slowly the Doctor opened his eyes. He now saw four green snouts, eight pale green eyes. He was sitting in a chair with arms; he moved his hands and feet slightly —there were no restraining straps or ropes. He looked up at the Draconians and managed a smile.

'How nice of you to invite me. Have I been spirited away to Draconia?' He looked about the room, noted the false impression of curved walls. 'No, I'd say this is the Draconian Embassy on Earth, tarted up to look like Draconia. Where's Jo?'

The Draconian First Secretary spoke. 'Your companion is still with your fellow Earthmen.'

The Doctor didn't bother to point out that he was a Time Lord and not an Earthman. 'Do you people realise what you've done? You've finally convinced them that we're both Draconian agents.'

'We know,' hissed the Draconian Ambassador, 'that you are both agents of the Earth Government, part of some plot against our Empire. You are working for General Williams. He hates our people. He is employing you to create tension among the people of Earth, to overthrow your own President, to bring the present crisis to a state of war.'

The Doctor looked up into the Ambassador's nostrils with astonishment. 'My dear chap, what a complicated mind you have. The ones trying to create war are the Ogrons—or at least the people behind them.'

Neither the Ambassador nor the First Secretary seemed to take the slightest notice of this last remark. The Ambassador continued, 'Tell me the details of the General's plot, so that I can expose him to your President. There is still a chance of peace. We have mind-probing machines just as efficient as those used by Earthmen. Either you speak now or we shall force you.'

'Can't you believe that you're on the wrong track?' asked the Doctor. 'There *is* a plot but the Earth people aren't behind it, any more than you are.'

The Ambassador stepped back. 'Take him away.' Two guards moved forward to grab the Doctor.

The Doctor smiled disarmingly. 'There's really no need to lay your claws on me, gentlemen. I'll go with you quietly.' Pretending to be about to rise from the chair, the Doctor suddenly thrust forward with his feet on the floor, pushed the chair over backwards, performed a somersault, sprang to his feet and darted for the french windows. One of the guards raised his blaster gun, its adjustment set to kill.

'No,' commanded the Ambassador. 'Don't shoot.'

The Doctor sprinted across a formal lawn, surprising an elderly Draconian gardener busy watering the flowers. Embassy guards gave chase, but the Doctor had a good start. He made for the concrete wall at the end of the lawn, scaled a tree, and dropped over the wall into the road outside the Embassy grounds. The road, lined with blank walls, ran as far as his eyes could see in a dead straight line. A small tubular hover-car, all black except for a chromium bumper, came hurtling down the road at high speed. The Doctor stepped forward and waved his hands to attract the driver's attention. As the vehicle approached he saw it had no driver. Only then did he realise it was making straight for him. He flattened himself against the wall. It pulled up directly in front of him, a mounted television eye on its roof turning to 'look' at him.

A metallic voice spoke. 'Get in.' A door in the side of the vehicle slid open.

'What if I refuse?' said the Doctor.

'You cannot refuse,' said the voice. 'You have nowhere to run to. Get in or be destroyed.' A slender tube on a stalk rose up from the roof of the vehicle, turned and pointed itself at the Doctor. 'You are an escaped prisoner. Escaped prisoners may be killed. It is an order.'

Defeated, the Doctor got into the hover-car. Instantly the door slid shut. He was a prisoner again.

Security guards flung open the door of the cell and pushed the Doctor inside.

'No more attempts to escape,' one of them growled.

'But I was kidnapped,' protested the Doctor. The door was slammed in his face.

Jo sat up from the bunk where she'd been trying to sleep. 'Doctor! What happened?'

Briefly he told her. 'The Draconians believe we're working for General Williams.'

'Oh no,' she groaned. Then she alerted. 'Do you hear that sound?' She put her fingers to her temples

61

as the strange sound increased.

'Is it the sound you heard on the spaceship?'

Jo nodded. Already it was affecting her mind. She fought to keep her thinking clear. 'Where's it coming from?'

Before the Doctor could answer they heard the firing of blaster guns in the corridor outside. Alarm bells clanged and the Security guards shouted, 'Draconians! We're being attacked! It's war!'

The two prisoners listened helplessly, trying to understand what was happening. All at once the crackle of energy from blaster guns ceased. Someone outside was operating the mechanism that locked the cell door. It opened. Two enormous Ogrons stood in the doorway. They were pointing their guns at the Doctor and Jo.

6

Prison on the Moon

'This is a military situation,' General Williams was saying. 'We should attack now!'

The President switched off her wall television screen. The news service had been showing pictures of the violent anti-Draconian riots. 'No, General. I will not be responsible for starting a war.'

She was tired, exhausted by the constant pressure of her office. For a moment she closed her eyes. Her mind went back to how the previous war between Earth and Draconia began. After much bitterness as to the exact line of the agreed space frontier, Earth and Draconian delegations were to meet on a neutral planet. She was young then, acting as aide to one of the senators selected for the Earth delegation. Young Lieutenant John Williams was a junior officer, responsible for communications. As they approached the planet, their ship ran into a neutron storm and was damaged. The ship's captain and all the senior officers were killed. Williams was left in command. For the young inexperienced lieutenant it was a terrifying responsibility: a damaged spaceship, full of important political Earth leaders. Just as he got the ship under control again he saw a Draconian vessel approaching. They expected to meet an unarmed civilian ship like their own; instead, the Draconian ship approaching was a fully armed battle cruiser. Williams could get no answer to his signals to the approaching ship. Convinced that the Draconians were about to attack, he blasted the battle cruiser with the retro-rockets of the unarmed Earth ship. The Draconians' power source exploded, disintegrating the battle cruiser and killing outright the entire Draconian peace delegation. The Earth ship was thrown clear. The Draconian Empire instantly declared war on Earth. It was a full-scale war of inter-stellar ballistic missiles and lasted three days, killing over five hundred million Draconians and Earthmen.

'I will not be responsible for starting a war,' the President repeated. 'We do not attack.'

'Madam President,' said the General, 'the Draconians are taunting us. They are even now using their Embassy here on Earth as a military base. Their First Secretary's trick in phoning you then kidnapping our prisoner, and now this latest outrage—an all-out attack by their Embassy guards on our Security Headquarters—are acts of war! If you don't act against them decisively you can and will be replaced. Your political opponents are clamouring for war.'

The President was faced with a problem. If she failed to please her people they would replace her; once out of office, she could never hope to achieve the good things that she wanted to do for Earth. 'I shall break off diplomatic relations,' she said. 'The Draconian Ambassador and his staff will be expelled from our planet. But unless you can give me conclusive evidence of Draconian war plans, I will not strike the first blow.'

'The proof we need is in the minds of those two traitors, Madam President. We shall have to use the mind probe.'

The President had once seen the mind probe used on a prisoner. She shook her head. 'Not on the girl, General. Perhaps I can persuade her to tell the truth. But as for the man, I give you permission to go ahead.'

The Doctor was firmly strapped in a metal chair, an iron skull-cap held on his head by tapes. The mind probe room was small, its walls brilliant red. The machine a simple black box with controls and a small television screen, occupied one corner. The General stood over the Doctor, issuing orders to the Security technician in charge of the apparatus.

'I shall ask you again,' said the General. 'How long have you been an agent of the Draconian Empire?'

'I am not, and never have been, anyone's agent,' replied the Doctor truthfully. 'Does this gadget really work?'

The General's face went scarlet. 'If we have to turn it to full power, you will wish you'd never been born. How did you get on the cargo ship?'

'In my own spaceship.'

General Williams nodded to the technician. 'More power.'

The technician turned a control and the General looked at the television screen. To his surprise he saw a blue oblong box floating through space, a flashing light at one end. The picture represented whatever was in the prisoner's mind. The General concealed his astonishment and turned back to the Doctor. 'Why did you help the Draconians attack the cargo ship?'

'I didn't and they weren't Draconians. They were Ogrons. They were also Ogrons, and not Draconians, who unsuccessfully attacked this prison after I'd escaped from the Draconian Embassy.'

Now the screen showed an Ogron entering the space cargo ship through the air-lock. The picture blurred, then was replaced by one of the Ogrons opening the door to the prison cell. As the amazed General stared, the Doctor and Jo were dragged from the cell down a prison corridor. Earth Security guards suddenly appeared in great numbers, counter-attacking the Ogrons, finally snatching back their two prisoners and forcing the Ogrons to retreat.

'These creatures that you keep producing in your imagination,' said General Williams, 'what are they?'

'Ogrons,' said the Doctor, bored by tiresome questions.

The General turned to the technician. 'Your machine can't be working correctly. Either that, or the prisoner can pretend to remember things.'

The technician looked worried. 'I've checked all the circuits, sir. What you see on the screen are definitely the prisoner's thoughts. Maybe he's been brainwashed, sir. Perhaps he believes what he's saying is the truth.'

General Williams considered. 'We must break through his conditioning. Step it up to full power.'

The technician hesitated. 'Full power, sir?'

'You heard my order.'

Reluctantly the technician turned the conrols of the mind probe. He was conditioned to have no feelings for prisoners, but he knew from experience that the full force of the mind probe could quickly destroy human brain cells, rendering a prisoner imbecile and useless for further questioning. 'It's now on full power, sir.'

General Williams looked closely into the Doctor's contorted face. 'Are you a Draconian spy? When do they plan to attack us? Who first recruited you? Who are the other Draconian agents on Earth. Answer! Answer!'

Waves of intense pain poured through the Doctor's mind. On the television screen only whirling patterns appeared. Using all his energy, the Doctor tried to overcome the pain. Then, suddenly, the mind probe machine blew a fuse. Smoke billowed out from it. The technician switched off immediately.

'General Williams,' said the terrified technician, 'I think he's destroyed the machine.'

Williams stepped back and regarded the helpless Doctor. 'Then we shall destroy him.'

Jo stood before the President's desk. 'But I keep telling you the truth. You just won't believe me.'

The President smiled. 'Sit down, my dear.'

Jo sat.

'Naturally you wish to be loyal to your friend,' continued the President, her voice kind. 'But your first loyalty is to Earth. Don't you want to help prevent a terrible war?'

'Of course we do. But someone else is trying to start it, not the Draconians.'

The President maintained her smile. 'How I wish I could believe you. But we have so many eye-witnesses to Draconian attacks. They've made *two* attempts now to rescue you from custody.'

'The first time was Draconians,' Jo admitted. 'But the second time it was Ogrons.'

The President shook her head regretfully. 'I am trying to help you, but you insist on these lies! The telephone flashed and she answered. 'Yes?'

A girl's voice said, 'General Williams to see you, Madam President.'

'Send him in, please.' She turned back to Jo. 'I can't help you if you won't help yourself.'

'I very much want to help myself,' said Jo. 'But you wouldn't believe my answers even if I gave them to you.'

General Williams entered through the round door. 'Madam President, the man's made a full confession. He's admitted they're both in the pay of the Draconian Secret Service.'

Jo was incensed. 'That isn't true! What have you done to him to make him say that?' She turned to the President. 'I want to see him.'

The President nodded to the guards by the door. 'Take her to the other prisoner. We shall talk again later.' She waited until Jo had gone. 'Well?'

General Williams sat down, defeated. 'He admitted nothing. I thought if I said that the girl might confess.'

He took a deep breath. 'We must use the mind probe on her.'

'No General. She's no more than a child. Perhaps there are other ways of getting the truth from her.'

'What other ways? Madam, if you won't let me use the mind probe——'

She raised her hand for silence. 'We could try kindness. It's that man's influence that's making her stick to her story. I want to talk to him, to try to make him see reason, for the girl's sake.'

The Doctor stood before the President's desk, flanked by armed palace guards.

'This is your final chance,' said the President, 'to tell the truth.'

'I have told you everything truthfully, Madam President,' the Doctor replied. He turned to General Williams. 'Sorry about your mind probe machine, old man.'

The General coughed and looked away.

The President continued. 'If it's a question of money, I will double any offer the Draconians made to you, and guarantee you and your companion freedom and a new identity on one of the colony planets.'

The General couldn't contain himself. 'Really, Madam President, this man's a traitor! We should make no trade with him.'

She politely ignored the outburst. 'Well, what do you say?'

'I can only repeat that I am not a Draconian agent, that so far as I know the Draconians do not intend to start a war, that the people who boarded the cargo ship were——'

She raised her hand. 'That's enough. We've heard it all before. Under the powers invested in me by the Special Security Act I am sending you to the Luna Penal Colony, the prison on the Moon.'

'Without a trial? With no chance to state my case? I thought Earth was a democracy.'

'The public trial of a Draconian agent,' said the President, 'will only increase the existing demand for war with Draconia. If at some later time you decide to help us by confessing everything, I may consider releasing you.'

The Doctor looked about himself. Surrounded by armed guards, there was no chance of escape from this place. 'What about my companion?'

'She will remain here,' said the President. 'Without your influence, I hope to make her see the error of her ways. General Williams, when is the next ship to the penal colony?'

'In half an hour, Madam President.'

'Good.' She turned back to the Doctor. 'This is your last thirty minutes on the planet of your birth, which you have tried to betray. You still have time to reconsider.'

The Doctor said, 'I don't wish to seem rude, Madam President, but since your mind is closed to anything beyond your immediate understanding, nothing that I say will be of the slightest interest to you. This is a great pity, since thousands of millions may die and two great empires will be destroyed through your unwillingness to grasp that I may have been speaking the truth.'

The General exploded. 'He's raving mad!'

'Then best that he go to the Moon,' said the President, averting her eyes from the Doctor's, 'for the rest of his life.'

7

The Master

The Doctor saw neither Earth nor the Moon on the short journey to Earth's satellite. The penal spaceship shuttle was windowless, a series of tiny cells just large enough for a prisoner to sit down, knees touching the metal door. From the ship the prisoners were shuffled through a narrow corridor that led directly into the prison. The Doctor's first sight of the Moon was when they were taken into a huge room with metallic walls, and here a big window looked out on to the bleak rocky moonscape, the airless world where any escaping prisoner would die instantly through lack of oxygen.

A Security guard lined the newly arrived prisoners against the wall facing the big window. Except for the Doctor, they all wore the prison uniforms issued to them before the journey.

'Don't move and don't talk,' said the guard before leaving.

The moment the guard had left, all the prisoners stretched and shuffled cramped feet. A young, fair-haired man with a keenly intelligent face turned to the Doctor. 'My name's Doughty. What did they get you for?'

The Doctor smiled. 'You'd never believe me.'

'But you're political, aren't you?'

This interested the Doctor. 'Are there many political prisoners here?'

Doughty shrugged. 'Who knows? The Government doesn't give away secrets! But yes—there's probably thousands here. Are you in the Peace Party?'

'You might say that I've been trying to stop a war.'

'Me too. I tried to sabotage a rocket launching base.'

As they talked the Doctor tried to take in his sur-roundings. Doors and corridors seemed to lead off from this large room in all directions. It was, he thought, some central area. Metal tables and chairs suggested prisoners could meet at this point. 'How long is your sentence?'

'Are you joking? When Security sends you to the Moon it's for ever. This is home for the rest of our lives.'

A stocky prisoner with short-cropped hair entered from one of the corridors. He wore the same drab grey prison uniform, though on his left arm was a bright red armband. He strutted up to the line of new pris-oners.

'All of you shut up and listen to me.' He shouted rather than spoke. A small bulge in Doughty's tunic pocket caught his eye. 'What have you got there?'

Doughty produced a small block wrapped in tin foil. 'Chocolate. My allowance from the remand prison.'

The man with the armband laughed. 'No chocolate allowed here, son. Give it over.' Without waiting, he snatched the little block from Doughty's hand.

The Doctor said, 'Do you realise that's stealing?'

'That's what I'm in for,' said the armband man. 'All of you, stand to attention! The Governor's going to speak to you.'

The prisoners made some attempt to stand to atten-tion as required. The Prison Governor entered, a tall man in black tunic and trousers. With him were four Security guards, all armed. He walked down the line of prisoners, eyeing them, then stopped to speak.

'I am the Governor of this penal colony. There is one rule here—to obey. If you behave you will be reasonably treated. If you misbehave you will be very badly treated. You are no longer people, you are things —my playthings. You have absolutely no rights, and there is no means of escape. Remember that you are here for the rest of your lives. Why isn't that man in uniform?'

The question seemed so much part of the speech that at first the armband man didn't react. When he did he sprang to attention.

'Don't know, sir. That's how they sent him.'

'See he's kitted out immediately,' said the Governor and left the room.

The armband man stepped forward. 'Now listen, all of you. My name's Cross, and that's my nature. I run a quiet, tidy section here. Any trouble from you and it's a black mark against me. So there's never any trouble. Got it?'

Doughty again spoke up. 'You talk as though you run this prison. Don't you realise you're really one of us? We're all victims of the system!'

'You,' said Cross, 'are making yourself highly eligible for the punishment block.'

But Doughty wasn't listening. His attention was riveted on an older prisoner who had just wandered in from one of the corridors. The newcomer had white hair and a long, sensitive face.

'Professor Dale,' said Doughty in awe.

Cross sneered. 'Yes, a real professor among us. You'll find a lot of your intellectual friends up here.' He spun round to the professor. 'This prisoner in the frilly shirt,' he shouted, indicating the Doctor. 'Get him kitted out double quick.' He turned away and strutted off down the corridor where the Governor had gone.

Professor Dale came across to Doughty, the man who had recognised him. 'Welcome to prison,' he said, wryly. 'You were on our Youth Committee, weren't you?'

The two men shook hands. 'That's right, professor. We met last year just before your arrest.'

'You'll be in good company here,' said the older man. 'I sometimes think there are more members of the Peace Party in this terrible prison than back on earth!'

'If I may ask,' said the Doctor, 'does anyone ever try to escape?'

The professor reacted with suspicion. 'Occasionally. Come with me. I'll get you a uniform.'

The Doctor hurried after Professor Dale. 'I was asking you a simple question.'

Dale did not reply until they arrived at a cupboard containing shelves of prison uniforms. 'Let's see,' he said, measuring the Doctor with his eyes, 'you're quite tall. I think you'll be size number fourteen or fifteen.' He reached up for a pair of trousers.

'Let me ask another question,' said the Doctor. 'What do we do all day here?'

'There is no day and no night. We're on the Moon. We go to bed when we feel like it. Food, that is to say tasteless soup, is served at regular intervals. We pass the time playing three-dimensional chess, listening to audio-books, pursuing handicrafts, and forming discussion groups. Try these on.' Dale offered the trousers to the Doctor.

'Do you ever discuss escape?' asked the Doctor, slipping off his own trousers.

'Of course not,' said Dale. He looked around uneasily. 'If you want to know, there was an escape attempt last month. The three men involved were all killed. Why are you asking about escape?'

The Doctor pulled on the prison trousers. They fitted fairly well. 'Because it's what I intend to do.'

'Are you a spy for the Governor, trying to draw me out?'

The Doctor looked at the man. 'If I were, I'd scarcely draw attention to myself so quickly.'

'A fine point of logic. Are you a member of the Peace Party?'

'I don't even know what it stands for,' said the Doctor. 'Tell me about it.'

Professor Dale sighed. 'We support the President's People's Party when it stands for peace. But when the President gives way to pressure from the warmongers, we oppose her. It's as simple as that. Let's find a jacket for you.' He hunted through the shelves for the right size. 'Since you don't seem to know anything about politics, why were you sent here?'

'Perhaps because I know there's a conspiracy to start a war.'

The professor showed no interest. 'We *all* know that, my dear man. Put this on.' He held out an ill-shapen grey jacket.

'I mean there is a third force at work,' the Doctor explained. 'The incidents between the two great Space empires are all faked. Would you like me to tell you about it?'

Professor Dale nodded. 'It would pass the time.' Then he smiled. 'After all, we've got nothing else to do.'

The President studied the two documents that General Williams had laid on her desk. Both carried the impressive emblem of Alderberan Four, a newly-created dominion within the Earth Empire. Both also carried photographs, one of the Doctor and the other of Jo. Under each photograph were details of these much-wanted criminals.

'There is no doubt about it,' said the President at last. 'These are the same two people. This explains many things, though I'm surprised about the girl. We shall have to hand them over.'

'But Madam,' said the General, 'they are in the pay of the Draconians. Surely we have prior claim to them? We still may extract vital information about the Draconians' war plans.'

'Relations with colony planets are always tricky, General Williams. If there is war, we'll need all our allies. These criminals must be very important to the

74

Dominion Government of Alderberan Four. I think we should co-operate. Bring in their representative.'

'If you insist, Madam.' General Williams crossed to the doorway and gave a polite signal.

The Master entered, wearing a uniform of a high-ranking diplomat of the Earth Empire. A vain man, he was particularly pleased how well the simple tunic of metallic orange fitted his athletic figure. He crossed to the President's desk, his short black beard jutting forward, eyes dancing, and bowed graciously.

'Madam President,' he said, 'this is indeed a very great honour. Allow me to present my credentials as Special Commissioner Master from your dominion planet, Alderberan Four.'

It was not the Master's first disguise in his long fight against the Doctor. Both renegade Time Lords, while the Doctor's long journeys through Time and Space had allowed him to help many Space species in need, the Master had used his wisdom and intelligence to spread fear and evil in his relentless quest for personal power.

With a flourish, the Master placed on the desk a document which he had forged with ingenious care. The President glanced at it, a mere formality.

'We have a problem,' she explained. 'These two people are already in our custody, one on Earth and the other in our penal colony on the Moon. We believe they are paid agents of the Draconians.'

The Master pretended amazement. 'These criminals? Still, I am not surprised. They will turn their hands to anything for money. However, Madam President, they are citizens of Alderberan Four, and we have sought them throughout the galaxy to bring them to trial for crimes on our planet.'

General Williams interrupted, 'But your planet is part of Earth's empire!'

'And has been granted dominion status,' the Master reminded him with a deferential smile.

The President interceded. 'He has a point, General Williams. Once a colony has been raised to dominion status, it enjoys certain autonomous rights, including the right to try and punish its own citizens.'

'If you concede to my request,' said the Master, 'we shall gladly return these people to you for interrogation once they have stood trial on Alderberan.'

'All right,' said the President. 'Your request is granted.'

The Master bowed deeply. 'I am most grateful to you, Madam President. May you live a long life and may energy shine on you from a million suns.'

Jo sat on her cell bunk facing the wall, playing mental games to avoid thinking about her fate.

Footsteps came down the passage outside, two or three men. She looked to the door, half hoping they were approaching her cell and half fearing them. The footsteps stopped and Jo nerved herself. The door opened and the Master stepped into the cell, smart in his diplomatic dress. Jo's mouth dropped open in astonishment. She had encountered the Master before in her travels with the Doctor. Yet though she knew of his evil, her immediate reaction was joy at seeing a familiar face. 'What are you doing here?' she exclaimed.

He smiled, flashing perfect white teeth. 'To coin a phrase, Miss Grant, I've come to take you away from all this.' The smile faded to show the joke was over. 'I am a fully accredited commissioner from a dominion planet within Earth's empire. You and the Doctor are two dangerous criminals, much sought for the crimes you have committed on my planet, and you are being handed into my custody.'

In fear, Jo pushed herself back on the bunk until her shoulders touched the cold prison wall. 'You're behind everything, aren't you? You told the Ogrons to attack those ships and pretend to be Draconians!'

'Quite correct, Miss Grant. A really exciting space-war will leave an inter-stellar power vacuum which I shall fill.' He offered his hand. 'May I help you up? We have a journey to make.'

'I'm not going anywhere with you?'

'Be reasonable, Miss Grant. You want to see the Doctor again, don't you? We're going to the Moon to collect him.'

'How do I know you're telling the truth?'

The Master shrugged. 'You'll only find that out by coming with me.' He offered his hand again. 'Well?'

Jo remained cautious. 'How did you know the Doctor and I were here, in this point in Time, in the first place?'

'Lucky chance,' the Master beamed. 'As you rightly said, I told the Ogrons to attack those cargo ships, Earth ships and ones from Draconia. I also devised that remarkably clever device which makes Earthmen see them as Draconians and vice versa. All the loot from the pirated ships the Ogrons take to their home planet, a most unpleasant and inhospitable place, but currently the centre of my operations. Much to my delight they brought back the Doctor's TARDIS.' He paused, clearly pleased with the success of his venture so far. 'Anything else you need to know?'

'Yes,' she said. 'Why do you want me and the Doctor to go with you?'

'A kindly impulse, Miss Grant.' His eyes twinkled. 'How can I, a fellow Time and Space traveller, leave you both to languish the rest of your natural lives in these awful prisons?'

'I don't believe that's your reason at all,' said Jo, easing herself up unaided from the bunk. 'But I suppose anywhere's better than this.'

'It is, Miss Grant, it is. Once Earth and Draconia get angry enough with each other, millions will perish in the first few minutes of the war. At least with me you two will be safe. Shall we go now?'

*

The Doctor had his first taste of prison soup and found it had no taste at all. Since the visit of the soup trolley a minute ago, all the prisoners sat quietly, some alone with their soup and their thoughts, others in small groups. The Doctor was with Professor Dale and the young man called Doughty. Dale, impressed by what the Doctor had to say, had brought Doughty into the conversation.

Doughty said, 'It's fantastic. Our seeing Draconians —Draconians seeing Earthmen. I can't believe it.'

Dale took his soup hungrily. 'Well I can. At last things make sense.'

'Thank you,' said the Doctor, keeping his voice low. 'You are the first person who's believed me.'

The professor continued. 'After the war we had years of peace with Draconia. In the past twenty years we've made trade treaties and many cultural exchanges. Then for no reason at all, these acts of piracy.'

Doughty tasted his soup and grimaced. 'Why should anyone try to start a war between the two empires?'

Before either the Doctor or Professor Dale could try to answer Doughty's question, their thoughts were interrupted by a shout.

'Hey! You over there!' Cross stood some distance from them, pointing at Professor Dale. 'Spot check. Over here on the double.'

Dale put down his soup bowl. 'Excuse me. One of our little prison rituals. Every now and then they decide to search us.'

As the Doctor watched with interest, Dale walked up to Cross and posed in what was clearly the approved stance for a prisoner about to be searched—feet apart, arms outstretched. Cross started to systematically feel Dale's uniform for anything that might be concealed on him.

Doughty turned back to his soup. 'It's humiliating to see a petty criminal like Cross in authority over someone like Professor Dale. I think I'll go mad in this place.'

But the Doctor didn't find the spectacle humiliating. On the contrary, he watched Cross and Dale with mounting interest. When Dale returned, the Doctor asked: 'What's happened?'

Dale picked up his soup bowl. 'What do you mean —what's happened? It was a routine search, that's all.'

'Come off it, man,' said the Doctor. 'I could see that fellow Cross talking all the time out of the side of his mouth. The two of you were giving off conspiracy in waves! What are you up to?'

Dale considered. 'An escape plan. It's now.'

Doughty was instantly alerted. 'How many going?'

The professor looked round to make sure no other prisoners were within earshot. 'Only two. We have to walk from the air-lock across the Moon's surface. There will be two space suits in the air-lock. We're going to steal some VIP spaceship that's just about to arrive from Earth.'

The Doctor asked, 'Who are you taking?'

'I'd planned to take another member of the Peace Party Central Committee with me. But now ...' Dale seemed to take a big decision. 'Doctor, I want you to come with me. We must get you back to Earth so that you can tell your story.'

The Doctor laughed. 'It was telling my story on Earth that got me sent here!'

'This time it will be different,' said Dale. 'We have important contacts everywhere. Journalists, broadcasters, even some friends in the Government. I'll make them believe you.'

Jo looked out at the bleak, forbidding moonscape as the Master's spaceship, which he had stolen from the Interplanetary Police, slowly sank down on to the illuminted landing pad. 'What are those domes?' she asked, pointing.

The Master glanced up from the instrument panel at the series of huge domes standing out from the rocky Moon surface. 'The prison, I imagine. What a wretched place to send people for the rest of their lives.' He chuckled, amused by the thought of other people's misery.

'Why are you always so nasty?'

'I thought I was charming!' He laughed, a quick, hard laugh.

'You are cruel and unkind and never think about anyone but yourself,' she said emphatically. 'You're bad and you know it.'

The Master touched one of the landing controls. The thrust of the retro-rockets increased to soften their landing. 'Miss Grant, try to see the overall picture. You can only have good people like the Doctor provided there are bad ones like me. So I provide a great service, don't you see?'

'You aren't answering my question.'

'Perhaps not. Shall we agree that I'm very ambitious?' A red light on the control panel flashed brilliantly. 'There, we've touched down. I'm going to be rather busy now presenting my credentials to the Prison Governor. I suggest we continue this interesting conversation some other time.'

The Doctor cautiously followed Professor Dale down a bare, metallic maintenance tunnel, leading away from the prisoners' main association area. He whispered in Dale's ear. 'Why is Cross helping you escape?'

'He's a petty criminal,' Dale replied, also in a whisper, 'but not really a bad man. I promised him that when the Peace Party comes to power on Earth, he will be released from this terrible place.'

'And he trusts you to keep your promise?'

'I have a certain reputation for honesty. Ah, here it is!' The professor stopped at an air-lock door. 'Let's see if he's kept *his* promise.' He tried the main handle of the heavy metal door. There was a click and the door swung gently open. 'After you, Doctor.'

The Doctor stepped into a small metal room with bare walls and another door at the far end. Two bright yellow space suits lay on the floor. Standing against the wall were two oxygen cylinder packs. Without speaking, the Professor closed the heavy door, bolting it firmly to ensure that it was airtight.

'Quick,' he said urgently. 'Get one of the suits. Cross gave me precise directions. We have a ten minute walk ahead of us on the Moon's surface. Then we'll be at the landing pad. In a few hours we shall be back on Earth.'

The two men started to pull on the heavy space suits.

Cross came soundlessly down the bare maintenance tunnel, keeping to the contour of the metallic wall. Standing at the far end of the tunnel, blaster gun at the ready, was one of the Prison Governor's personal guards, just in case anything went wrong. It was the Governor's proud boast that no prisoner had ever escaped and that most of those who tried died in the attempt, a fact that deterred the majority of prisoners from even contemplating a break-out. To maintain an atmosphere of futility, a few of the trusted guards were under instructions to co-operate with occasional escape attempts, then help to kill the escapers.

Cross had now reached the closed door to the air-lock. He took a quick glance through an inspection panel set in the door, turned to the waiting guard and gave the thumbs-up sign. The guard nodded. Cross silently slid over the bolts on the outside of the door.

The Doctor and Professor Dale had on their space suits. Dale said, 'Clip my cylinders on to the back of my suit, Doctor, then I'll fix yours.'

The Doctor picked up one of the cylinder packs, reacted to its lightness. 'This is empty.'

'It can't be ...' Dale picked up the other cylinder pack, felt how light it was. 'There's some mistake.'

'I don't think so.' The Doctor dropped the pack he was holding, crossed to the door that led to the maintenance tunnel. He slid back the bolts and tried to open the door. 'It's locked from the outside.'

As he spoke they both heard a hissing sound. Dale looked startled. 'What's that?'

'They're depressurising,' exclaimed the Doctor. 'They've let us get ourselves in here without oxygen, and now they're pumping all the air out!'

'We'll suffocate!' Dale, white with fear, crossed to the bolted door, pounding it with his bare fists. 'Help! Let us out!'

'You're wasting your breath,' warned the Doctor. 'They'll never hear us. In any case, I don't think they want to.'

8

Space Walk

'I don't like it,' said the Prison Governor, still scrutinising the Master's forged credentials. 'Normally no prisoner leaves here, at least not alive.'

The Master stood respectfully before the Governor's desk. They were in the Governor's private office, a large metal-walled room. The only decoration was a three-dimensional colour portrait of the President on the wall behind the Governor's desk.

'I have permission from the President herself,' said the Master. 'You see her signature there.'

The Governor sighed. 'Very well.' He handed back the Master's papers. 'But is seems odd to me. I'll have the prisoner brought here.' He reached for his videophone.

'Couldn't I be taken to him?' asked the Master. 'I want to see his face when he realises that at last I've found him.'

The Governor paused. 'Yes, no reason why not.' He smiled at the idea. 'What sort of crimes has he committed on your planet?'

'Fraud, theft, the usual enterprises of the criminal mind.' The Master made a move to the door. 'Perhaps someone could show me the way? . . .'

'There's no hurry, is there? I thought you might care for a spot of refreshment before you make your arrest.' The Governor laughed. 'I can assure you, the prisoner isn't going to run away!'

'It's most kind of you,' replied the Master. 'But after such a long search, you can imagine my eagerness to lay hands on the man.'

'Just as you like.' The Governor touched a button

on his videophone. A guard's face appeared on the little monitor screen. 'Escort needed for special visitor to L block. On the double.'

Professor Dale lay gasping on the floor, his face blue. The doctor leaned against the air-lock door, using his last strength to bang one of the empty oxygen cylinder packs against the heavy metal. Then, involuntarily, the cylinder pack slipped from his hand and fell noisily to the floor. The Doctor looked through the inspection panel, a last hope that someone outside might have heard his tapping. For a moment he had the impression of seeing a swarthy, bearded, smiling face that was all too familiar to him. As unconsciousness seeped into the edges of his mind, he wondered why he had imagined seeing the Master, his deadly rival. It was a strange delusion for his last moments of life. With that thought he slumped to the floor, prepared for death.

The door opened. A rush of air filled the room. The Doctor breathed deeply, believing he was already dead and this was some after-life that he'd never been too sure about. Heavy footsteps were pounding the metal floor all around him, and now hard hands were grabbing his shoulders, raising him.

'Having a nap?' asked the Master, bending over the Doctor. 'What a good thing I happened to drop by. I'd hate you to come to any harm.'

The Doctor was yanked to his feet and marched off towards the Governor's office to be released into the Master's custody.

Jo was frightened and bored at the same time. For over an hour she had waited in the Master's police spaceship, cooped up in a caged corner of the hold. This caged area—two walls of solid metal hull and two

walls of iron bars with a locked gate set in one of them
—was at least more comfortable than her cell in the
great Security Headquarters prison on Earth. It had
two bunks, each with mattress and blankets. Neverthe-
less, it was another confinement, and she was tired of
being locked up. Her mind turned idly to canaries
and budgerigars who spend their entire lives in cages.

Then she heard sounds reverberating through the
metal body of the spaceship. She listened intently,
turning her attention to the air-lock door through
which the Master had gone when he went to visit the
Prison Governor. The door opened, and to her delight
the Doctor entered.

He smiled. 'Jo, how are you?'

Before she could answer, the Master followed the
Doctor. With him came two guards in black uniforms,
holding blaster guns on the Doctor's back.

'You'll have plenty of time to exchange pleasantries
on our journey,' said the Master. He turned to the
guards. 'Put the prisoner in the cage, then you can
leave him to me.'

The Master locked the air-lock door. 'An interesting
reversal, don't you think, Doctor? Once upon a time
you came to visit me when I was in prison. What a pity
you found out about my little conspiracy with the
Sea-Devils.* With their help I could have enslaved the
whole of your precious planet Earth!'

'A good thing you were stopped,' said Jo.

'In retrospect, Miss Grant, perhaps you are right.'
The Master's eyes twinkled mischievously. 'I might
have learnt to be content with Earth alone, whereas
now I am after something a million times bigger.'

'No doubt to control the Universe.' The Doctor
smiled.

'Even I have my limitations,' bantered the Master.
'But shall we say this galaxy, the Milky Way?'

* See *Doctor Who and the Sea-Devils.*

'Tell me,' asked the Doctor, more seriously, 'why am I still alive?'

The Master laughed. 'We Time Lords live to immense ages.'

'You know what I mean, why have you gone to all this trouble to retrieve me alive from that prison?'

'Believe it or not, Doctor, your health is very precious to me—at least for the moment. My employers are very interested in you.'

'Your employers?' said Jo, curiously. 'The Ogrons?'

The Master's smile faded. 'Please, Miss Grant, I employ *them*.'

'Whatever you're up to,' said the Doctor, 'you'll get no help from me.'

'I don't need it, thank you. Your presence will be enough. Now, if you'll excuse me, I have some rather complicated astro-navigational calculations to make. We are about to go to the outer extremity of the galaxy, to the home planet of our friends the Ogrons.'

'Why are you taking us there?' asked Jo.

The Master's smile returned. 'That, my dear Miss Grant, you will discover when you arrive. Believe me, I have a big surprise in store for you.' He turned to leave them, then paused. 'Please don't try to escape. You'll find it's quite impossible. What's more, a television eye will be watching you in your cage at all times. From where I shall be sitting at the ship's controls, I shall be able to see you at any moment. Have a happy journey.' With a cheery wave the Master left the hold, making his way for'ard towards the ship's flight deck.

The moment the Master had gone, the Doctor inspected the lock on the gate set in the cage wall. He shook his head. 'No chance of picking that.'

'What about your sonic screwdriver?' asked Jo.

'The Master took it off me at the prison, when they gave me back my own clothes. Anyway, we don't want to

86

escape just yet.' He settled back on to one of the bunks.

'But why not? I'm tired of being cooped up like an animal!'

'You heard the Master, Jo. We're going to the Ogron's planet. He says that's where the TARDIS is.' He leaned back, cradling his head in his hands. 'We wait till we're well under way, then we escape.'

'How?'

'With this.' From its hiding place under the back of his jacket collar, the Doctor pulled out a string file. It looked like a very thin necklace.

'What about the television eye? He's going to be watching us.'

'Then he mustn't see anything to worry him. We'll set to work as soon as we've taken off.'

'Just as you say, Doctor.' Once again Jo sat down to wait.

On the flight deck the Master completed his navigational calculations. His hand on the control that would start the ship's powerful motors, he paused to consider how his plans were going. It was unfortunate that the Doctor had accidentally turned up at the same moment in Time when the Master hoped to seize total power over the millions of suns and planets of the Milky Way. Still, he had so far turned the situation to his advantage. His allies, whom he personally loathed and despised, would be delighted to have the Doctor turned over to them as prisoner. He could see them in his imagination, gliding forward to take a closer look at his catch, chattering in the soulless, metallic voices.

'Stupid pepper pots!' he said to himself with a grin. 'Stupid Daleks!'

He gently moved the control. The engines roared into life as the ship rocketed from the Moon's surface, and into the endless blackness of Space.

*

The Doctor and Jo lifted themselves from the floor of the cage, where they had been thrown by the force of take-off.

'He could have warned us,' said Joe, tenderly feeling a bruised knee.

'Well he didn't.' The Doctor glanced towards the television eye, sure that once they were in flight the Master would be making his first visual check of the two prisoners.

Jo said, 'Do you think he's watching? You said that once we were under way——'

The Doctor *herrumped* loudly, pretending to clear his throat. 'So I said to the High Council of the Time Lords, they had no right to put me on trial to begin with——'

Jo stared at him. 'Doctor, what are you talking about?'

He moved so that he was standing with his back to the iron bars, his face well in view of the television eye. ' "If I choose to spend my time wandering round the Universe," I told them, "that's my business." '

Now Jo understood. The Doctor was using the string file on one of the bars behind his back; his body masked what his hands were doing from the television eye.

She spoke up, in case the Master was listening. 'What happened then?'

'My fellow Time Lords found me guilty of meddling in the affairs of other species, changed my appearance and exiled me to Earth. That's when I met you.'

The Master's voice came over a hidden loudspeaker. 'Doctor, do you really have to bore Miss Grant with your reminiscences?'

The Doctor glared towards the television eye. 'I think it most improper of you to eavesdrop on our conversation.'

'So do I,' said Jo, loudly. 'Kindly stop listening to us.'

They heard the Master chuckle. 'Just as you please, Miss Grant.'

'Where was I?' said the Doctor, his hands still working feverishly behind his back.

'Being exiled to planet Earth,' said Jo. 'I'm fascinated by your story.'

With no further interruptions from the Master, the two prisoners continued their mock conversation, in the hope that the Master would not notice what the Doctor was really doing. While the Doctor continued to work the string file round one of the bars of the cage, Jo busied herself ripping open the mattress on one of the bunks. To keep the conversation going the Doctor talked about his special attachment to the United Nations Intelligence Taskforce and his feelings about UNIT's British Commander, Brigadier Lethbridge Stewart. 'I soon realised that the trouble with him was that he'd got a military mind.'

'Hardly surprising,' said Jo, 'since he's a military man.'

'That's just the trouble. Hide-bound, you see. He always wants to do everything by the rules. He doesn't realise there are times when you simply have to *cut through* the red tape.' The Doctor could feel that he had taken the string file right through the bar behind him.

'And you've managed to cut through?' asked Jo, not sure whether she had understood the Doctor's secret message.

'Yes,' he replied, working the string file into another position. 'But you have to cut through not only at the bottom, but also at the top.'

They continued this masquerade for another ten minutes, then the Doctor said, 'Well, I'm tired. It's time I got some rest.'

'You can rest at a time like this?' asked Jo.

'Why not? There's no point standing around when I can lie down.' In a whisper the Doctor added, 'Just let's hope he isn't watching now!'

The Doctor turned round, lifted aside the severed bar, then wriggled through the gap. Jo took the bar from him.

'Your jacket!' she whispered urgently.

'Sorry, almost forgot.' Outside the cage, the Doctor quickly shrugged off his long jacket and shoved it through the bars to Jo. 'See you—I hope.' He disappeared down the ship's main corridor.

Jo first wedged the bar back into position, using bits of torn cloth from the mattress to hold it in place. Then she pulled the stuffing from the mattress and pushed it down one of the sleeves of the Doctor's jacket.

The Master was absorbed in a treasured copy of H. G. Wells's *War of the Worlds*. Before turning the page of his book, he glanced up at the television monitor screen that showed his prisoners. The girl, Jo Grant, was now sitting on one of the bunks, hugging her knees and talking. The Master turned up the volume of his loudspeaker to listen.

'... I'm always telling you, Doctor, you've got no real idea where you're going in that TARDIS. I mean to say you were supposed to be getting me back to Earth, and all we do is land in one terrible situation after another. And what's the Brigadier going to say? After all, I'm supposed to be working for UNIT——'

The Master switched off the loudspeakers. The Doctor appeared to have taken to the other bunk, his form clearly discernible under the blankets. For a moment the Master alerted, suspecting a trick—was that really the Doctor or some dummy they had made? Then he noticed the sleeve of the Doctor's jacket protruding from the blankets and felt at ease.

His momentary fears at rest, the Master turned the page of his book and continued to read. With the spaceship on automatic pilot, he had nothing else to do.

Keeping well out of sight of the television eye, the Doctor had found a locker containing a space suit. He quickly put it on, checked the oxygen cylinder pack, and returned to where Jo was keeping up the pretence of talking to his reclining figure.

'... Anyway, if we ever do get back to Earth, I'm never coming up in that TARDIS again ...'

The Doctor caught Jo's eye. She gave an almost imperceptible nod to indicate that she had seen him. He gave her the thumbs-up sign then opened the inner door to the air-lock.

From the corner of her eye, Jo saw the Doctor disappear into the air-lock. She realised his intention must be to space-walk along the outer hull of the spaceship and enter the flight deck from the outside, thus taking the Master by surprise. All she had to do was continue the pretence that the Doctor was still in the cage with her.

'I suppose it's my own fault, really,' she said, desperately trying to think what to say next. 'If I hadn't persuaded my uncle to pull strings and get me a job I'd never have got mixed up with UNIT. Some people think intelligence work is all very romantic, all glamorous dinner parties with James Bond types. Instead, I'm either filing letters at UNIT Headquarters or I'm off with you in some ghastly place being chased by monsters ...'

The Master's voice broke in over the loudspeaker. 'Doctor—Miss Grant—you'd better hold on. I'm about to make a rather sharp course correction. It could give you both a bit of a jolt.'

Jo looked at the air-lock door in horror, realising that if the Doctor was already outside the ship, a sudden jolt could send him tumbling away into the depths of Space, lost for ever.

9

Frontier In Space

Weightless now that he was outside the spaceship, the Doctor worked his way slowly along the hull towards the flight deck, using hand-holds which some thoughtful designer had provided for the purpose. All at once he became aware of a great glare of light from the rear end of the ship. Without thinking he turned to look, holding on with one hand. Too late he realised the glare was caused by a suddenly increased burst from the rocket motors. The hull of the ship lurched away from him and the Doctor found himself swimming in Space.

Vibrations from the rocket motors shuddered through the metal walls of the flight deck. Carefully watching the control dials, the Master eased back the rocket motor lever. The vibrations stopped. The spaceship was once again gliding freely. The Master looked up at the television monitor, where he saw Jo release her grip on the iron bars.

'Everything all right, Miss Grant?'

'Yes,' she replied, her voice hollow with fear for what had happened to the Doctor. 'I'm fine.'

'And how are you, Doctor? No ill effects, I trust?'

The form under the blankets didn't move.

'Please don't wake him,' said Jo. 'He's gone to sleep.'

The Master turned off the loudspeaker, stroked his beard thoughtfully. How, he wondered, could the Doctor have slept through the vibrations caused by the course correction?

With sudden decision, he reached for his blaster gun, got up and made his way aft towards the prisoners' cage.

The distance between the Doctor and the spaceship had widened considerably. The Doctor's natural inclination was to 'swim' back to the hull, but in airless space this was impossible. The Master had but to give one further short burst from the rocket motors, and the Doctor would be parted from the spaceship for ever.

Then he got an idea. The basis of rocket propulsion in the vacuum of Space was that the release of energy in one direction caused the source of that energy, for instance a spaceship, to move in the opposite direction. Quickly he reached to the oxygen cylinders strapped on his back and uncoupled the main tube that led to his helmet, taking care to hold his breath like an underwater swimmer, and to hold his thumb over the end of the tube. He pointed the tube away from the spaceship and gently raised his thumb. At that moment precious oxygen was escaping into the void. But slowly, at first imperceptibly, he started to drift back towards the spaceship. His lungs bursting, he re-coupled the tube, hoping that the drift would continue under its own momentum. With terrifying slowness he reached the spaceship and grabbed one of the hand-holds. A few moments later he was standing by the external door of the flight deck. Looking through a port-hole he saw the captain's seat empty and the door aft closed. It meant he could open the external door without robbing the spaceship of its entire oxygen, which would have killed Jo and the Master. As he prised open the external hatch it crossed his mind as odd that the Master had deserted his command position.

*

Jo kept up her conversation with the dummy of the Doctor. 'You see, Doctor, you really shouldn't take such risks. You're not as young as you were, over seven hundred years old according to you, and one of these days your luck will run out——'

The Master's voice cut in on her monologue. 'Very touching, Miss Grant, but you can drop this masquerade now.'

She jumped. On the other side of the bars the Master stood pointing his blaster gun. With a cunning smile he reached through the bars and ripped away the bunk blankets, revealing the Doctor's dummy. 'Now, young lady, where is the Doctor?'

There was no use pretending. 'He found a space suit and went outside.'

The Master laughed. 'What a prosaic expression! He went outside, indeed. No doubt to check the weather?'

'To get at you,' she said, with as much venom as she could muster. 'I imagine he's making his way towards the flight deck.'

The Master unlocked the gate set in the bars. 'Come out.'

Jo stayed where she was. 'Why?'

'Because I'll blast you stone dead if you don't, Miss Grant. It may not have occurred to you, but although the Doctor may be useful to me, you are totally useless. There are men with an eye for a girl with a pretty face, adventurers with a touch of pity for the innocent victim of a situation. I am not one of those men.' His voice became menacing. 'Come out of that cage in five seconds or stop existing!'

Jo came out of the cage. 'What now?'

'Down to the air-lock.' The Master prodded Jo with his blaster gun. 'Get in there!' He swung open the air-lock door, pushed Jo inside, closed the door and went to stand where the television eye could see him. 'Already on the flight deck, Doctor? Miss Grant is inside the air-lock. Unless you surrender immediately I shall open the outer door of the air-lock from the control here. Miss Grant will be sucked into space——'

His concentration focused on the television eye, he failed to notice when the Doctor crept along the corridor from for'ard. With a quick chop, the Doctor knocked the blaster gun from the Master's hand. The Master whirled round to face his adversary.

'What an ingenious fellow you are, Doctor.'

The Doctor, who had discarded his space helmet on the flight deck, commanded, 'Release Miss Grant from the air-lock.'

The Master looked down at his blaster gun on the floor. Catching the glance, the Doctor kicked the gun further away. The Master licked his lips nervously. 'Just as you say, Doctor——'

Feigning surrender, the Master suddenly spun round to the Doctor with a clenched fist. The Doctor staggered backwards, but regained balance in time to catch the Master by the neck. The Master drove his elbow into the Doctor's stomach, but ignoring the pain, the Doctor slammed a heavy blow at the side of the Master's head. The Master reeled towards the air-lock and fell to the ground, apparently almost unconscious. Then he sprang nimbly to his feet and put a hand on the control that operated the outer air-lock door. 'Kick that blaster gun across to me,' he screamed, 'or we say goodbye to Miss Grant!'

'You couldn't do that.'

'Want to try me? I shall count to three. One ... two ...'

The Doctor kicked the blaster gun down the corridor. It stopped at the Master's feet. He picked it up.

'Thank you, Doctor. At last you are beginning to show some sense——'

A profound clang vibrated through the entire ship. While they fought and threatened, some other craft in

Space had locked on to the Master's spaceship.

'We have company,' observed the Doctor. 'Your Ogron friends?'

The Master looked distinctly worried. 'No. I've no idea who it is.'

'Then I suggest you be hospitable, old chap. We are probably heavily outnumbered.'

As they watched, the air-lock door slowly opened. Jo, white-faced with fear, came out first. Immediately behind her was a Draconian Space captain. The Doctor went quietly up to the Master, relieved him of the blaster gun and put it to one side.

'Welcome,' said the Master, though his voice was a little hoarse. 'To what do I owe the pleasure?'

The Draconian captain looked along his green snout at the humanoids. 'Why have you violated the Draconian frontier in Space?'

'I apologise most deeply,' answered the Master quickly. 'My prisoners tried to escape. They caused the ship to be thrown off course.'

The Draconian captain gave a short hissing sound. Then he spoke again. 'Disputes between Earthmen are not my concern. Owing to the many insults and provocations against the Empire of Draconia, a state of emergency has been declared. Diplomatic relations with your empire no longer exist. You have violated Draconian Space. The penalty is death. I shall take you to our planet where you will be executed in public.'

Two Draconian soldiers trained their blaster guns on the three prisoners through the bars. A Draconian flight crew was now in command of the Master's spaceship, heading it full speed towards Draconia.

'Personally, I'm quite happy to go to their planet,' said the Doctor. 'I shall tell the Emperor what you have been trying to do.'

'You really think he'll believe you?' sneered the Master.

'It won't be my first visit there,' the Doctor replied. 'I was able to help them once when they were in trouble.'

'How good of you,' the Master scoffed. He turned to Jo, 'It astounds me how you can put up with him, he's so sickeningly *good*.'

Jo turned away, ignoring the Master.

'Oh well,' he said, 'if we're going to get huffy with each other, I might as well catch some sleep. Call me when we get there.' He lay down on one of the bunks, rolled over to face the wall. Unseen by either the Doctor or Jo, the Master produced from his tunic pocket a tiny black box and pressed the button on its side. A light in the box began to flash off and on.

A million miles away across the vastness of Space, a speck of light on a monitor screen flashed off and on in the flight deck of an Ogron spaceship. One of the two Ogrons at the controls noticed the flashing light and pointed.

'Him call for help.'

His companion, a huge Ogron with arms thick as most Earthmen's thighs, turned to look at the screen.

'Him call—we go!'

Working great clumsy levers, the Ogron captain boosted the ship's rocket motors to full speed.

On the Planet of Draconia, the Prince strode into his father's great throne room at the Royal Palace. He was glad to be back home after his time as Draconian Ambassador to Earth. With the recent severance of all diplomatic relations between the two Empires, he and his staff had been forced to leave the Earth Embassy.

The Emperor, his green flesh wizened with age,

looked up in surprise. Even his own son was required to seek an audience before speaking to him.

'So, father,' said the Prince as he entered, 'once again the Earthmen have invaded our Space!'

The Emperor hissed, then spoke in a fragile, high-pitched voice. 'You will address the Emperor in the proper manner.'

The Prince obediently took a step back and bowed. 'Your pardon. May I have permission to address the Emperor?' He mounted the three steps to the throne and kissed his father's claw. 'My life at your command.'

The old Emperor nodded, satisfied now with his son's behaviour. 'One day you will be Emperor. Then you will appreciate the importance of formality.' He paused, drawing in air through his nostrils. 'Yes, I am aware that an Earth ship crossed the agreed frontier in Space. Prisoners from that ship are being brought to me.'

'Surely we shall now declare war upon Earth,' said the Prince. 'Let me lead your battle fleet to crush them!'

'They too have battle fleets, my son. Such a war could bring down both Empires.' The Emperor had never forgotten the enormous loss of Draconian life in the last war with Earth.

'Not if we strike first,' replied the Prince with enthusiasm. 'Then we shall be the victors.'

'In such a war there are no victors.'

'But father,' implored the Prince, 'the nobles of the Court are demanding action. The throne depends upon their support. Emperors have been disposed of before when they displeased the great Draconian families.'

The old Emperor was silent. Although the position of Emperor passed from father to son, he knew from Draconian history that weak Emperors in the past had been suddenly, sometimes violently, removed from office, when they lost the support of Draconia's nobles.

'I shall question these Earthmen myself. I have already sent for them.'

'And waste more time listening to their lies?'

The Emperor looked keenly into his son's eyes. 'Sometimes I think you might be the first to depose me.'

'Never! I am your willing servant, father. I only wish to warn you——'

A Court official hurried into the throne room. 'May I have permission to address the Emperor?'

The Emperor nodded.

'The prisoners, sir, have arrived.'

'Then let them be brought in,' replied the Emperor.

The official hurried out.

'They are bound to lie to you,' said the Prince. 'They'll want to save their own lives.'

'We shall see,' said the Emperor. 'We shall see.'

The captain from the Draconian battle cruiser that had caught the Master's ship over the frontier came in with the Doctor, Jo and the Master. 'I bring the prisoners, sir.' Five armed guards entered behind the trio, blaster guns held at the ready.

The Doctor stepped straight towards the throne. 'May I have permission to address the Emperor?' He took a step closer, hand held out to take and kiss the Emperor's claw. Three of the guards stepped forward.

'Wait!' said the Emperor. He waved the guards aside.

'Thank you.' The Doctor took the Emperor's claw and kissed it. 'My life at your command.'

The Draconian Prince was outraged. 'This is an insult! He mocks our ways!'

The Doctor turned to him. 'Don't I know you from Earth? You were the Draconian Ambassador there.'

'How dare you address the Emperor in the manner reserved for nobles of Draconia!'

'I *am* a noble of Draconia,' said the Doctor. 'The rank was conferred on me by the fifteenth Emperor.'

The Prince hissed loudly. 'The fifteenth Emperor reigned five hundred years ago!'

The Master saw his opportunity to step forward. 'Your Majesty, do not be taken in by so absurd a story. This man is a dangerous criminal.'

'Be silent!' The Emperor raised his claw angrily. Then he turned to the Doctor. 'There is a legend of one from Space who assisted the Emperor of five hundred years ago at a time of great trouble. But you cannot be that person. No Earthman lives so long.'

'The man you speak of, Your Majesty, was he not known as the Doctor? Did he not help your people overcome a great plague which came from Space?'

The Emperor nodded, scratching his snout. 'That is the legend.'

'The race from which I come lives longer than any Earthman, Your Majesty. Moreover, we have the power to travel both in Space and in Time. Believe me, I am the Doctor.'

'Even if I accept your claim,' said the Emperor, 'you have broken our laws. Why did you violate Draconian Space?'

'If I may explain, Your Majesty,' said the Master, before the Doctor had time to reply, 'this man was— and still is—my prisoner. Perhaps I can show you my credentials——'

The Doctor cut in. 'It is true I was brought here as a prisoner, Your Majesty. Yet I came here willingly. This man, who pretends to be some Commissioner from one of Earth's dominion planets, is behind a plot to provoke war between Earth and Draconia. He is a renegade of my own race, and he is using creatures called Ogrons to attack your ships and those of Earth.'

The Master laughed. 'He is not only a criminal, Your Majesty. He is also mad!'

'Ogrons?' said the Emperor. 'It was Earthmen who have been attacking our spaceships. They have been seen many times.'

'No,' cried the Doctor, 'your people have seen Ogrons, who appeared to them as Earthmen because of an hypnotic device.'

Jo piped up, 'It's true, Your Majesty. And when Ogrons attacked Earth ships, Earthmen saw them as Draconians.'

The Prince hissed very loudly. 'Silence! No female may speak in the presence of the Emperor.'

Jo said, 'What a stupid rule. Still, anything to oblige.'

'If what you say is true,' said the Emperor, 'it would explain much. We have lived in peace with the Earthmen for many years. Then, suddenly, they began to raid our spaceships. When we protested they said we were attacking their ships.'

The Prince said, 'Was that not to cover up their own attacks?'

The Emperor ignored his son's remark. 'Doctor, what action do you suggest?'

'Meet with the Earthmen. Combine with them to discover the truth.'

The Court official hurried back into the throne room. 'May I have permission to address the Emperor?'

'Yes?'

The official bowed. 'Your Majesty, an Earth spaceship seeks permission to land in the palace space port. By radio they say they are on a special mission from the President of Earth.'

'This is a trick,' said the Prince. He looked up to his father's throne. 'I implore you not to allow them to land! We should rather blast them from our sky!'

'I will hear what their President has to say,' said the Emperor. 'I grant my permission.'

The Court official bowed and hurried away.

'Thank you, Your Majesty,' said the Doctor. 'Only if Earth and Draconia will work together can we arrive at the truth.'

'I also wish to applaud Your Majesty's wisdom,' said

101

the Master, who seemed more cheerful since news of the impending arrival of an Earth spaceship. 'No one could be more devoted to peace than I am. As a commissioner for Earth's Interplanetary Police, I have devoted my life to the cause of law and order, which can only be maintained in a state of peace.'

The Doctor grinned, 'Are you feeling all right, old chap?'

'Only in a time of social and international stability,' the Master went on, ignoring the Doctor, 'can society deal with criminals such as this man and this unfortunate girl.'

'What cheek!' Jo exclaimed. She pulled a face. 'Oh, sorry, I forgot that mere females aren't allowed to speak in His Majesty's most regal and high-and-mighty presence, so I'll try and control my natural tendency to expect to be regarded as an equal even though I am just a girl——'

'Silence!' screamed the Prince.

The Prince's protest was drowned by the roar of a spaceship landing in the Palace grounds.

'Once that ship has landed,' said the Doctor, 'we'll see who is the real criminal.' He turned to the Master. 'They'll check up on those phoney credentials of yours, you know.'

'I await the arrival of my colleagues with the utmost confidence,' the Master replied. 'Believe me, once they are here all my problems will be over.'

As the Master spoke, Jo started to hear the strange humming sound. 'Doctor, listen. That sound!'

The Prince roared at her, 'Be silent, female!'

'Be silent yourself! Doctor, it's the sound the Ogrons make.'

The Doctor nodded. 'Your Majesty, I fear something may be very wrong. The ship that's just landed in your grounds, I beg you to place it under guard immediately.'

'Under guard?' said the Emperor. 'A moment ago

you wished me to receive this special mission from the President of Earth.'

'The Doctor's changing his tune,' said the Master, very sure of himself now. 'He knows that justice is at hand.'

'Your Majesty,' said the Doctor, 'please take warning——'

But he was too late. From outside the throne room they heard the crackle of blaster guns. The guards surrounding the Doctor and Jo turned to the entrance, in time to be shot down by a mob of six invading Ogrons.

'Soldiers from Earth!' shouted the Draconian Prince. 'This is war!'

'They're Ogrons,' screamed Jo. 'And don't tell me to shut up.'

'They are Earthmen,' said the Prince, firing at the Ogrons with a small blaster gun plucked from his sleeve.

The Doctor grabbed Jo's arm. 'Don't stop to argue. Get out of the crossfire!'

The Master saw the Doctor propelling Jo to a point of safety behind the Emperor's throne. 'Get them,' he shouted at the Ogrons. 'Get my prisoners.'

But other Draconian Palace guards had now entered the battle, outnumbering the Ogrons. The Doctor looked out from their point of hiding. 'They're being driven off, but the Master's getting away with them.'

'Then let him go,' said Jo.

'My prisoners,' shouted the Master, now nearing the door to escape. 'You must get them. That is a command.'

A huge, lumbering Ogron caught sight of the Doctor's head and marched across to him, shooting down a Draconian guard in the way. Another Draconian opened fire on the Ogron and he turned to fire back. The Doctor seized his opportunity to attack. Coming up behind the Ogron he applied a Venusian Karate hold to the monster's thick neck. With painful slowness, the Ogron sank to his knees and finally fell in a faint on the floor. The Doctor looked up to find himself surrounded by menacing Draconian guards. The other Ogrons, with the Master, had disappeared. From the Palace grounds came the roar of a spaceship taking off.

The Prince looked up to his father. 'Now will you believe in the treachery of Earthmen? They attacked our palace to rescue their agents.' He turned to the guards surrounding the Doctor. 'Destroy him!'

The guards raised their blaster guns to kill the Doctor.

'No!' screamed Jo, with such power that even the guards paused to turn to her. 'Your Majesty, what do you see lying on the floor here?'

Forgetting the rule that no female might speak in his presence, the old Emperor looked at the prostrate Ogron. 'I see one of your Earth soldiers, though why your companion attacked him I do not fully understand.'

'Because he is *not* an Earth soldier,' said the Doctor. 'Jo, can you still hear that sound?'

She listened. 'Yes, but it's fading. It's almost gone.'

'Your Majesty, I beg you,' said the Doctor. 'Look again.'

The Emperor blinked and turned back his gaze to the huge form lying unconscious on the throne room floor. The strange sound no longer affected his mind and he saw what he believed to be an Earth soldier turn into an Ogron. 'Do not destroy him,' he said, indicating the Doctor who was still threatened by Draconian blaster guns. 'He has spoken the truth. Now we shall listen to more from him.'

10

The Verge of War

The Master sat at the controls of the Ogrons' spaceship as it zoomed away from the Planet of Draconia. 'Not a bad operation,' he said to the Ogron seated in the co-pilot's position. 'But unfortunately you bungled the most important part. You allowed the Doctor to escape.'

'We rescued you,' mumbled the Ogron. 'That important.'

The Master laughed. 'To me *and* to you! Without me you wouldn't have enough brains between you to make a wheelbarrow. Anyhow, there is one consolation. The Draconian Emperor is now convinced of the wickedness of Earthmen. With any luck he'll have the Doctor executed.'

A second Ogron entered the flight deck, his thick-set semi-human face twitching with worry. 'I count us,' he said, as though this conveyed all that was on his mind.

'Marvellous,' said the Master. 'Soon you'll learn to read.'

'I count us,' the Ogron repeated. 'One of us is missing.'

The Master turned. 'Missing where?'

'He left behind. Doctor got him.'

The Master's face was suffused with anger. 'And you let it happen? You great dolts! Once the hypno-sound has faded the Draconians will know who really attacked them.'

'What must we do?'

'There's only one thing we can do,' replied the Master. 'The Doctor and his captured Ogron must never reach Earth.'

*

The Ogron captured by the Doctor lay bound hand and foot on the throne room floor, a Draconian guard standing over him. Conscious now, the Ogron's eyes darted from the guard to the trio at the foot of the throne steps, the Doctor, Jo and the Prince. He was terrified they would torture him now that he was helpless.

'Have you come round, old chap?' The Doctor crossed to the Ogron. 'Why does the Master want war between Earth and Draconia?'

The Ogron replied, 'We obey the Master.'

'It hasn't done you much good, has it? Did he ever explain why he wants to start a major war?'

'We obey, not ask.'

The Draconian Prince called from where he stood near the throne. 'Did you attack our spaceships and those of the Earthmen?'

'We obey.'

'I shall use the mind probe on him,' announced the Prince. 'That will force him to talk.'

'You'll be wasting your time,' said the Doctor. 'The Ogrons have the greatest defence of all—stupidity. He hasn't got a mind *to* probe!'

'I should like to ask something,' said the Emperor in his fragile, high-pitched voice. 'Why did that sound make us see this creature as a soldier from Earth?'

'Because you're frightened of the people from Earth,' said Jo.

'Be silent, female!' roared the Prince. 'Draconians fear nothing.'

'Don't be silly,' she retorted. 'Of course you do. You fear them and they fear you. That's why when Earthmen heard the sound, they saw Draconians.'

'It's true,' said the Emperor. 'We both fear each other.'

'And fear breeds hatred,' said the Doctor. 'Fear leads people into war.'

The Emperor slowly, thoughtfully, nodded his head. 'As happened before with the terrible cost of life. We shall tell the Earthmen what has happened here. They too must know the truth.'

'They will not believe us,' said the Prince.

'Your son is right,' added the Doctor. 'Therefore I suggest a special mission be sent to Earth. 'We can take the Ogron as evidence.'

The Prince hissed. 'You imagine a Draconian ship can cross the frontier in Space now without being destroyed by the Earth ships? You forget that the two empires are on the verge of war.'

'Then we can use the ship the Master brought us in,' said Jo. 'It's an Earth police spaceship.'

'I have warned you,' said the Prince, cold with anger. 'Females are not permitted to speak.'

The Emperor raised his claw. 'The female may speak. We must respect the peculiar customs of our guests.' He turned to Jo. 'Your suggestion has merit.'

'Thank you,' she replied, then turned to the Prince. 'See!'

The Emperor continued to speak. 'You, Doctor, will go with this mission. And you, my son, will lead it.'

Jo made her way down the spaceship's main corridor to the cage where she and the Doctor had been held prisoner. She carried a container of food for the Ogron who now stood glaring angrily through the bars at his Draconian guard. To Jo's relief she saw that the Draconians had clamped a new bar into position to replace the one the Doctor had cut away with his string file.

'I've brought you something to eat,' she announced. 'This is going to be a long journey to Earth.'

She offered the container at arm's length. The Ogron reached out a hairy fist and snatched it. He prised open the lid, picked an item wrapped in tin-foil and put it down his mouth.

'You're supposed to unwrap the stuff first,' Jo warned. But the Ogron had already swallowed and was now stuffing his mouth full with another item from the container, tin-foil and all. Jo turned to the Draconian guard. 'You want to be careful. They're not as stupid as they look.'

The guard ignored her.

'All right,' she said. 'I know—females are not allowed to speak. I can't imagine how you treat your poor wives.' She turned and went to the flight deck where the Doctor was piloting the ship.

The Draconian guard, bored by his task of watching over the ape-like creature in the cage, crossed to a port hole and looked out. While the guard had his back turned, the Ogron took the opportunity to match his strength against the bars of the cage. Exerting great force he fractionally bent two bars, widening the gap between them.

The guard turned back from the port-hole. The Ogron slunk into a corner, innocently taking further items from the food container. The Earth girl had said they were in for a long journey. With any luck, the Ogron hoped, the Draconian guard would stop watching over him long enough for a renewed attack on the bars.

Jo returned to the flight deck. 'Where are we now?'

The Doctor looked at the ship's instruments, made a rapid mental calculation. 'Just about to cross the frontier into Earth's Space.'

She was pleased. 'That's good.'

'Unless your Earthmen destroy us,' said the Draconian Prince uneasily.

The Doctor smiled. 'We're in an Earth police ship, remember, even if it is stolen.'

The Prince was staring at one of the radar screens. 'What's that?' He pointed to a small blob of light on the screen.

The Doctor studied the blob of light. 'It's another

spaceship. They seem to be following us. I wonder what it can be?'

In the control cabin of the Ogrons' spaceship the Master was also studying a blob of light on his screen. 'That must be them,' he announced to the Ogrons standing round. 'No other ship would be on course for Earth at a time like this.'

An Ogron spoke up, '*We* are on course for Earth.'

The Master sighed with exasperation. 'Because we are following them, you idiot. Now shut up and let me concentrate.' In his head he did a sum to work out the relative speeds of the two ships. 'Soon we shall be in striking distance.'

'What you will do, Master?'

'I'd like to take the Doctor alive, if I can. But if not I shall blow him to pieces. A pity, really.'

'You not wish kill him?'

'Of course I do, you fool,' said the Master. 'But to use rocket fire at long range, somehow it lacks the personal touch! When he dies I want to see the surprised look on his face.'

The Doctor, Jo and the Prince all concentrated on the radar screen. The light blob was very large now.

'They're closing in,' said the Doctor. 'It may be a frontier patrol ship coming to investigate us.'

Jo said, 'Can't we talk to them by radio, say who we are?'

The Doctor nodded. 'We can try.' He looked about the controls for the radio-telephone equipment, pulled a microphone close to his lips. 'This is Earth police spaceship'—he noticed a plate pinned over the instrument panel; it carried a number—'2390, on a special mission to the President of Earth. Do you read me?'

*

The Ogrons clustering round the Master grinned. One of them voiced their feelings. 'You very lucky, Master. Out of bigness of Space you find right ship.'

'This isn't luck,' said the Master scathingly. 'I worked it all out. Once they realised they'd got one of you lot as prisoner, their first thought would be to take him to Earth to show the President. Then they'd realise that a Draconian space ship entering Earth Space at this time would be destroyed out of hand, so they would use the Earth police ship that I inadvertently provided them.'

One of the Ogrons frowned, deep furrows appearing on his sloping primitive forehead. 'How you know all this when you not talk to them?'

'I just explained, I worked it out! This is like playing a game of chess.'

'Chess?' repeated the Ogron.

'Oh, forget it!'

The Doctor's voice came over the loudspeaker a second time. 'I repeat, this is Earth police spaceship 2390. Do you read me?'

The Master turned to speak into the radio microphone. To the astonishment of the Ogrons, he spoke with a voice entirely different from his own. 'This is Earth police spaceship 142. Your ship is one that has been reported stolen. You will please reduce speed so that we can board you.'

An Ogron asked, 'How you make voice different?'

'Because I'm a genius,' replied the Master.

The Doctor again spoke into the microphone. 'Police spaceship 2390 to 142. We have recaptured this ship and are taking it to Earth.'

Over the loudspeaker a voice answered. 'Reduce speed so that we can board you.'

'Why should we submit to this delay?' said the Prince. 'Our mission has diplomatic immunity.'

'Unfortunately they don't know that,' said the Doctor. He turned to the microphone. 'We are reducing speed as you request.'

Jo looked worried. 'Doctor, we don't know that it's really the police.'

He nodded. 'Exactly, Jo. I want to get them into the range of the visual scanner.'

The Doctor activated controls that fired one of the forward rocket motors for a five second burst, slowing the spaceship by thousands of miles per minute.

'Now,' he said, turning to the controls that operated the external television eyes of the ship, 'let's see if we can pick them up on the screen.'

On the monitor screen a spaceship could be seen in the distance. The Doctor adjusted the controls, so that the picture zoomed in on the spaceship.

'It's the Ogrons!' Jo exclaimed.

A blinding flash of light glared on the ship's starboard side as a rocket-missile exploded. Half closing his eyes to reduce the glare, the Doctor moved the ship's directional controls. The ship dived steeply while at the same time swerving to one side. Jo and the Prince were thrown to the floor.

The Draconian guarding the Ogron prisoner also saw the reflection of the exploding missile. He turned to look at the port hole. For a few seconds the missile burnt like a tiny sun. Then, without warning, the floor gave way as the Doctor made the ship dive and swerve. The guard crashed heavily against the metal wall. He crumpled in a heap, unconscious. The Ogron, also thrown about by the sudden change of direction, slowly got to his feet. With the guard knocked out he had nothing more to fear. He took two bars of the cage in his great hands and wrenched them apart. Then he stepped through the opening to freedom and lumbered for'ard towards the flight deck.

Jo and the Prince were back on their feet, looking with the Doctor at the screen. The Ogrons' spaceship, though still visible, was a considerable distance away.

'I think we're shaking them off,' said the Doctor. 'The Master's not a very good pilot, you know. Now let's see how fast we can go!' He put his hand on the accelerator.

Jo screamed. 'Doctor! Watch out!'

The Doctor turned, saw the Ogron coming straight at him. 'Keep out of the way, Jo! Go to the hold— you'll be safe there.'

The Ogron hurled himself at the Doctor, trying to grasp him in a crushing bear hug. The Prince rushed forward, dug his claws into the Ogron's neck, and tried to pull him away from the Doctor. As the three 'men'—Time Lord, Draconian, Ogron—crashed to the floor, the Prince's elbow accidentally touched the control. A two second burst of energy directed forward halved the ship's speed.

The Master and his Ogron companions watched the Earth spaceship becoming larger on their screen.

'They're slowing,' said the Master. 'We must have hit them.'

The Ogron co-pilot asked, 'I fire again? Make big fire all round them.'

'No. Perhaps we can take the Doctor alive after all. Prepare a boarding party.'

Jo was kneeling by the unconscious Draconian guard. 'Please try to wake up,' she pleaded. 'You could help fight the Ogron.'

The Draconian slowly opened his eyes. 'Where am I?'

'On a spaceship going to Earth, and you let the Ogron escape. Can you get to your feet?'

The Draconian guard remained dazed. 'Big flash of light, then darkness.'

'If you can't move, tell me how to use your blaster gun. I'll get it for you.' She reached to where the gun lay on the floor.

The Draconian's reaction was automatic, a reflex from military training never to allow someone else to touch his weapon. His claw shot forward, snatching up the blaster gun.

'Then you go and use it,' said Jo. 'But please do something quickly to help the Doctor and your Prince.'

The Draconian focused his eyes on the bent bars of the cage. 'Creature—escaped.'

'That's right.' Jo realised she was going to get no help from him. 'Can you stand up?'

'I try.' The Draconian slowly struggled to his feet.

'Let me help you.' Jo took one of the Draconian's arms, but he shook her away.

'Females do not help.' As he spoke, he sank to the floor again, eyelids flickering.

At that moment Jo heard the now familiar clang of another spaceship locking on. Instinctively she looked up at the air-lock door. In panic she saw that it wasn't locked on the inside. She scrambled to her feet to get to the door and bolt it. As her hand went forward to slide home the first bolt, the door opened and an Ogron loomed over her. Fear kept her rooted to where she stood. The Ogron lurched forward and grabbed her round the waist, dragging her into the air-lock. She was aware of the sight and smell of the other Ogrons coming through the air-lock, invading the spaceship.

*

On the flight deck the Doctor had finally managed to get a stupefying Venusian Karate hold on the Ogron's thick neck. The Ogron slowly sank to his knees, unconscious, and the Doctor carefully lowered him to the floor.

'We've been boarded,' the Doctor shouted to the Prince. 'Find weapons.'

The Prince didn't have to be told. He was already opening lockers and cupboards in the hope of finding blaster guns. 'Here,' he said, having found what he was looking for, 'take one of these.' He handed over an official Earth Interplanetary Police blaster gun just as the first boarding Ogron arrived at the doorway to the flight deck.

The Master waited impatiently in the safety of the Ogrons' spaceship flight deck. 'What's happening? They should have overpowered everyone on board by now. Must I do *everything* myself!'

As he stood up to go and check how the boarding party was getting on, the Ogron co-pilot pointed to the monitor screen. 'Master, something come.'

He stopped to look. An Earth battle cruiser was fast approaching the two locked-on spaceships. 'Well, I'll be ...' He started issuing orders. 'Recall the boarding party. We'll unlock as soon as they're back on board.'

On the Earth spaceship, the Doctor and the Prince with their blaster guns had proved more than a match for the Ogrons. Growling in anger at the burn wounds inflicted on them, the Ogrons retreated down the corridor to the air-lock, dragging with them the Ogron put unconscious by the Doctor's karate hold. They jostled each other to get through the air-lock door, tumbled into their own ship, closed *its* door, and immediately unlocked from the Earth ship.

In a howling wind, all the air inside the Earth ship escaped through the open air-lock. Both the Doctor and the Prince, gasping for breath, were sucked bodily into the hold in time to see the semi-conscious Draconian guard sliding along the floor towards the gaping air-lock door. The Prince threw himself to the floor, hooked a leg through the bars of the cage, and grabbed the guard's leg. Meanwhile the Doctor worked his way from one secure hand-hold to another until he had reached the door. For a second he found himself looking into the emptiness of Space. Then he slammed shut the door and sank to the floor, his lungs bursting. With the air-lock door closed once again, the ship's air pressure sensor automatically started to pump in air from the high-pressure tanks.

'We'll be all right in a minute or two,' said the Doctor, at last able to breathe. Then he realised what had happened. 'Jo! They've taken Jo!'

Planet of the Ogrons

A giant Ogron pushed Jo up the corridor of the Ogrons' spaceship and into the flight deck, twisting her arms behind her back.

'We get girl, Master.'

The Master, preoccupied with piloting the ship away from the approaching Earth battle cruiser, remained some moments looking at the control dials. Then he turned to face Jo. 'Well, I suppose you'll have to do, Miss Grant, though I did rather want the Doctor.' He looked up at the towering Ogron. 'You blundering oafs, why didn't you get him?'

'He shoot with gun.'

'Obviously he didn't shoot with a blow pipe——' He stopped mid-sentence as a burst of static came over the loudspeaker. 'Everyone shut up. I want to listen to this.' He increased the volume.

A voice said, 'This is Earth battle cruiser X-29. Identify yourself.'

The Doctor's voice replied. 'This is Earth police spaceship 2390. We are on a special mission to the President.'

'Identify the ship that has just unlocked from you. They do not answer my signals.'

The Master chuckled. 'Of course not, you twit!'

The Doctor's voice came again over the loudspeaker. 'You must pursue and capture that ship immediately. It is of vital importance——'

But the other voice spoke over the Doctor's. 'You are in possession of a stolen police spaceship. You are under arrest, whoever you are. Stand by to be boarded. Do not offer any resistance.'

The Master looked up at Jo, his eyes twinkling. 'This is the best radio show I've listened to in years. Aren't you enjoying it?'

'I repeat,' said the voice from the Earth battle cruiser, 'you are under arrest. Stand by to be boarded.'

'Very well,' came the Doctor's voice. 'We are standing by.'

The Master switched off the loudspeaker. 'Poor Doctor, enmeshed in the toils of bureaucracy. It'll take him some time to talk his way out of *that*.'

'But he'll get to the President,' said Jo. 'He'll tell her everything.'

'You think she'll believe a word of it?'

'She will when she sees the Ogron prisoner,' Jo replied pertly. 'He's our evidence.'

'What a shame,' said the Master. 'Your so-called evidence is standing behind you.'

Jo turned as best she could. She was surrounded by Ogrons. 'I don't believe you.'

'I know they all look alike, Miss Grant, so you'll have to take my word for it.'

Jo had another idea. 'The Draconian Prince knows the truth and he's still with the Doctor!'

The Master stroked his beard. 'My dear Miss Grant, in the climate of opinion and tension which I have created do you think that anyone on Earth will believe the word of a Draconian? Unfortunately for you, everything is now going my way.'

'Surely we cannot be expected to believe this preposterous story!' General Williams spoke emphatically.

The others in the President's office stared at him—the Doctor, the Draconian Prince and the President. Even though diplomatic relations between Earth and Draconia had been severed and the two empires were on the brink of armed conflict, the presence of the

117

Emperor's son called for a certain politeness.

The General realised his bluntness may have gone too far. 'I'm a military man, not a politician. I speak my mind. What the Doctor says about this man called the Master and about Ogrons is very difficult to believe.'

The Prince held back his head, snout protruding pugnaciously. 'I confirm everything the Doctor has told you. My word should be enough.'

'Indeed, yes,' said the President, tactfully. 'But to convince my people I shall need concrete evidence. Earth is a democracy. I cannot tell my people what to think.'

'There's only one thing for it,' said the Doctor. 'We must mount an expedition to find the planet of the Ogrons. The proof you need is there.'

'Let us be sensible,' said the General. 'With Earth almost at war, how can we divert our forces into such a pointless expedition? Suppose this is yet another Draconian trick, to divide our strength?'

The Prince started to hiss with anger, but before he could say anything the Doctor spoke. 'I'm not asking for a battle fleet, General Williams. One small space ship is all I need.'

'Then your request is granted,' said the President.

'On the contrary,' cut in General Williams. 'Your request is denied.' He turned to the President. 'In military matters, Madam President, your authority is limited. Such an expedition needs *my* consent.

The Prince hissed again with mounting rage. 'How can we expect help from a man such as this General? Many years ago he deliberately caused war between our peoples.'

'That is untrue,' the General retorted.

'You destroyed a Draconian ship that came on a mission of peace.'

'A ship that was about to open fire on us, when we were damaged and helpless!'

The Doctor tried to intervene. 'Gentlemen, please, let us talk of the future, not the past.'

The President raised a hand to silence the Doctor. 'No, I want these things to be said. It's time everything was discussed openly. Well, General Williams, what made you think the Draconian ship was about to open fire on you?'

'They didn't answer my signals, that's why!'

'The communications equipment of the Draconian ship,' said the Prince, 'had been destroyed by the same neutron storm that damaged your ship. I have read records of my father's Court. What I say is the truth.'

There was a moment's silence while General Williams digested this shattering news.

'I was not to know that,' he said at last. 'But tell me, why did you send a battle cruiser to meet a peace mission? The agreement was that both ships should be unarmed.'

'Naturally we sent a battle cruiser,' replied the Prince. 'How else should a Draconian nobleman travel? But it's missile banks were empty. The ship *was* unarmed.'

The General's face paled. 'If this is true, then I am solely responsible for starting a war that killed millions of people, Earthmen and Draconians.'

The Doctor felt he must now intervene. 'May I suggest, sir, that fear and suspicion was the cause of your war? And that the whole terrible bloodshed is going to happen again unless we do something about it pretty quickly!'

The General turned to face the Draconian Prince. 'Your Highness, please accept my deepest regrets for the wrong I have done your people.'

The Prince bowed his head in acknowledgment. 'We must all try to forget the past, General Williams.'

The General now turned back to the President. 'Madam President, as your military adviser may I recommend that we adopt the Doctor's plan to seek and find the planet of the Ogrons?'

The President smiled and nodded approval. 'Agreed, General Williams.'

'Furthermore,' he continued, 'if I may be temporarily relieved of my immediate duties, I wish to lead this expedition myself.'

'Certainly,' said the President. 'I know that if this planet exists, you will find it.'

'And you will accompany me?' the General asked the Doctor.

'Gladly,' said the Doctor. He hesitated. 'There is one request I wish to make to you, Madam President.'

'Yes?'

'As a visitor to your great empire, internal politics are not my concern. But on the Moon you have thousands of prisoners, many of them good people whose only crime was that they believed in peace. If war is averted will you release them?'

The President considered. 'Doctor, if we can eliminate the threat of war we can also live in peace among ourselves. In a secure peace I imagine my Government would rather have those people here on Earth, contributing their skills to our society, than exiled to the Moon.'

'Thank you, Madam President. Well, General Williams, shall we begin?'

The Ogrons' spaceship made a hard, bumpy landing in a devil's playground of rocks and boulders. Jo, one wrist held in an Ogron's vice-like grip, was yanked down the main corridor to the exit. She looked out on to the forbidding landscape of black rocks and grey sand.

'There's no place like home,' she said wryly.

The Ogron grunted and led her away from the spaceship. The Master and a group of Ogrons were ahead of them, making for a cave in the side of a cliff.

'We not home yet,' said the Ogron. 'Home good, inside hill.'

'It sounds cosy.'

Inside the cliff was a labyrinth of crudely fashioned passageways and open areas, lit by flickering torches from the rough rock walls. At one point they passed an Ogron suspended from the rocky ceiling by heavy chains.

'Him bad Ogron,' Jo's guard explained. 'Stole food from holy place.'

'How long's he going to hang like that?'

'Till too weak to run. Then we give him to big lizard.'

Jo shuddered.

At last they were in a fairly large cave, the Master's quarters. Against the rough walls were various items of advanced communications equipment. The Master was seated in a comfortable swivel chair. 'Welcome to my humble abode, Miss Grant.'

She looked round the place. 'You must have been more comfortable the time on Earth you were in prison.'

'These are temporary quarters. I shall soon change them for something better.'

'You'll soon be back in prison again,' she replied. 'Once the Doctor convinces everyone of the truth, Earth and Draconia will combine their space fleets to attack you.'

He shook his head. 'I doubt it. There is too much mutual distrust.'

'The Doctor will find you somehow.'

He smiled. 'I hope he does. In fact, he must come here, not only to find you but also to try and get back his beloved TARDIS. Look in that corner.'

Jo stared into a gloomy far corner of the cave. Her eyes now accustomed to the flickering torch light, she saw the TARDIS standing there. 'Well, you'll be sorry when he gets here.' It was all she could think of to say.

'On the contrary, Miss Grant. I *want* him here. To achieve that, I'm going to set a trap for him, and you are going to help me.'

Jo said nothing.

'What's this, Miss Grant? No noble speech to say that you'd rather die than do anything to harm your precious Doctor?'

'You know that I'm never going to help you. If you're going to set a trap you can do it with your stupid Ogron friends.'

'And if I should force you?'

Jo nerved herself. 'If you want to hurt me there's nothing I can do to stop you.'

'Exactly, Miss Grant. I've tried hypnotising you before now but you fail to respond.' He glanced round at the electronic equipment in the cave and his eyes settled on a small, dull grey box with various knobs and controls. 'My hypno-sound device, perhaps? I could terrify you with illusions that you were seeing Drashigs and other monsters.' He picked up the box lovingly. 'Ingenious, don't you think?'

'Is that how you made Draconians see Earthmen?'

'And Earthmen see Draconians! Yes, entirely my own creation.' He put the box down. 'But I doubt that would work on you a second time. So we may have to use cruder methods to persuade you to help me trap the Doctor——'

A tall Ogron entered the cave. 'Master, I bring news.'

The Master looked up. 'What is it?'

'Two of our raiding ships come back. They find two Earth cargo ships. One fought back. They smashed it.'

The Master smiled. 'Excellent! There *must* be war now!'

Waiting for General Williams to prepare his spaceship, the President, the Doctor and the Draconian Prince watched a flash newscast on her television wall. 'Two more Earth cargo ships have been intercepted in Earth Space by the Draconians,' said the newscaster. 'Mass rallies are demanding war with Draconia.' The picture cut to a shot of Congressman Brook addressing a crowd of thousands. 'I warn the President that we shall no longer tolerate these murderous attacks! I hear cries from all sides—Attack Draconia! Attack now! There is only one final solution and that is war, war, war!' The crowd went mad in a frenzy of cheering, then in unison chanted the word, *'War!'*

The President switched off the television wall and turned to the Doctor and the Prince. 'I don't know how much longer I can hold them. The thought of war always excites people.'

'When they have so much to lose?' said the Draconian Prince. 'Even their own lives?'

'When in history have people thought about that, Your Highness? People enter war always thinking that they will win, and that they personally will survive.'

The Prince threw back his head. 'On Draconia meetings such as these'—he indicated the blank television wall—'would not be permitted. Only noblemen may express opinions.'

'Our nations are very different,' said the President. 'Earth prefers democracy, but that in itself creates problems. Give me proof about the Ogrons, and I shall speak to the people of Earth and convince them that Draconia has had nothing to do with these attacks on our cargo ships——'

General Williams entered the President's office. 'Madam President, everything is ready. We shall take my personal scout ship.'

The Prince took the President's hand and kissed it. 'May you live a long life and may energy shine on you from a million suns.'

The President replied formally, 'And may water,

oxygen and plutonium be found in abundance where-ever you land.'

The Prince continued to hold the President's hand in his green scaly claw. 'My life at your command,' he said with meaning, something he would normally have said only to his father the Emperor.'

'And mine at yours,' she said, moved by the Prince's words. 'Now go, the three of you, and may your mission be successful. The future of two great empires depends on you.'

The Doctor bowed to the President and hurried away with the Prince and General Williams.

The Trap

Jo sat on the hard earth floor of her cell in the Ogron stronghold and tried not to cry. It was bad enough being in the great soulless Security Prison on Earth: at least then there had been a chance that someone might have listened to her. But now she was a prisoner of the real enemy—the Master who was wholly evil, and the stupidly savage Ogrons. What's more, she was convinced the Master would use torture to make her help him defeat the Doctor in some way. Being placed in this cell was part of some demoralising preparation, to give her time to think about what was to come.

She could see no means of escape. Two walls of the cell were solid rock; the other two 'walls' consisted of heavy iron bars from floor to the cave roof. A cage door was set in the bars, its huge primitive lock secure. Next door was another cell, empty and its door standing open. Jo looked longingly at the open cage door. Then as a thought struck her, she inspected the floor at the foot of the dividing iron bars. The bars between the two cells came down to a heavy iron girder that simply 'sat' on the hard earth floor. It would be possible to burrow under the girder and get into the next cell, like a rabbit burrowing under a wire-mesh fence. She started scratching at the earth but quickly realised it was too hard packed for her to make any impression. She looked at her torn bleeding fingers in despair.

Someone was coming. She heard the heavy pounding of an Ogron's feet approaching down the rock-walled corridor. Instinctively she cowered to the back of the cell, fearing the torture was now to begin.

A single Ogron came into the flickering light. He carried a wooden bowl and earthenware jug. He stopped at the gate to her cell, produced a massive iron key and let himself in. 'You eat.'

Jo came forward and took the bowl. It contained a substance like gruel, so stodgy that the spoon stood upright in it. 'Thanks.'

The Ogron rubbed his stomach. 'Food is good.'

'Fabulous,' she said.

'You eat good, get big, become Ogron wife.'

'There's a thought,' she answered. 'Well, I'd better fatten myself up.'

'Eat, get big.' He put the jug of water down beside her, relocked the door and went away.

The food in the bowl had no taste at all. Then she suddenly realised that the spoon was made of strong metal. She put down the bowl, went back to the bars dividing the two cells and tried to scrape away the earth using the spoon. The hardness of the earth again defeated her efforts and she sank back on her haunches in despair. Then another thought came to her. She poured a little of the water on to the hard-packed earth. When she tried again to use the spoon she found she could move away some of the softened earth.

The General's personal scout spaceship was one of the most advanced the Doctor had ever travelled in. A dozen Earth soldiers sat in a special compartment aft set aside for the General's personal bodyguard. On the flight deck were the Draconian Prince, the Doctor, General Williams and the ship's pilot. The Doctor was busy making calculations on a memo pad.

'In thirty-four seconds,' he told the pilot, 'make a course correction to galactic co-ordinate 2349 to 6784.'

The pilot looked to General Williams for confirmation.

Williams nodded. 'Do whatever the Doctor says.' He turned to the Doctor. 'You realise this course will take us into a completely uninhabited sector of the galaxy?'

'It'll take us to where we'll find the Ogrons' planet.'

The General looked less than convinced. 'May I ask where you obtained this information?'

'From the Master,' replied the Doctor. 'He fed the co-ordinates into his ship's computer when I was his prisoner.' He turned to the Draconian Prince. 'When you captured the ship I extracted the information from the ship's memory banks.'

The Prince spoke. 'The female with whom you travel, the one who talks, you expect to find her on this Ogron planet?'

'That is my hope,' said the Doctor.

'I hope so too,' said the Prince. 'You must educate her to be silent, then she will be a very nice person.'

The Doctor suppressed a smile.

Jo reckoned she had scraped away enough earth to make her escape. Lying on her back, gripping the heavy girder, she pulled herself head first into the dip. To her delight her head went easily under the girder, and with a further heave she brought through her shoulders. Now half of her was on the 'free' side of the dividing iron bars. She raised herself on her elbows and wriggled until she was in a sitting position—sitting in the dip. Her legs protruded up into the locked cell. Since knees only bend backwards, she had to turn over on to her stomach to draw her legs through. She struggled to her feet, aware that both the back and front of her clothes were plastered with mud. She stepped out of the unlocked cell and tried to remember how she had been brought here from the Master's private quarters.

A minute later she realised that she was lost in the maze of tunnels and passages. Standing at an intersection of four corridors, she saw that the end of one led out into a more brightly-lit area. She ran in that direction.

Here there was a profusion of flickering flares on the walls. It was a big cave, the rock walls more smoothly cut than anywhere she had seen since her arrival. At one end a mound of rubbish lay under what appeared to be a wall drawing. Curious, Jo went closer to the great picture on the wall. In crude shapes, which she presumed was the best one might expect from an Ogron artist, the wall drawing showed a huge animal like a lizard, or one of Earth's prehistoric dinosaurs, holding something in its claws. She went closer and saw that what it held was in fact an Ogron, a tiny figure dwarfed by the size of the monster.

The sound of footsteps made her race to a place of hiding in the shadows. As she watched an Ogron entered the brightly-lit area carrying an armful of strange fruit or vegetables. He walked up to the picture and spoke to it.

'O Great Mighty One, I bring you food. Eat well of what we give. Allow us to share your planet. Do not eat Ogrons.'

With the final words of the incantation the Ogron threw the food on to the pile that Jo had thought was rubbish. He fell to his knees, crossed arms over his chest, rocked forward three times, then got up and backed away.

Jo waited until the Ogron had gone, then emerged from the shadows and continued her search for the Master's quarters.

General Williams's pilot pointed to a disc on the ship's monitor screen. 'That's it, sir. I'll bring it into better view.' He adjusted a control and the disc grew in size until it filled the screen. 'The planet you wished to reach, sir.'

The General looked up from the records he had been studying during the journey. 'According to the Galactic Survey, Doctor, this planet is uninhabited. It has no valuable minerals and very little vegetation. There is one dominant life-form—a large and savage lizard. Since it is such a miserable and unpleasant place, neither Earth nor Draconia has ever colonised it.'

'There you are, then,' said the Doctor. 'Just the place the Ogrons would choose as a base.'

The Prince asked, 'If they are on this planet, how do we find them?'

'When we get in closer,' said the Doctor, 'we'll have to keep looking until we see some signs of life.'

'Go into close orbit,' the General ordered his pilot.

'We must search for these lizards,' said the Prince.

'Why?' queried the General. 'We're supposed to be hunting Ogrons.'

'Ogrons would know enough to hide,' said the Prince. 'Lizards will not. If the lizards are savage perhaps they eat Ogrons. So where we see lizards, we can be sure the Ogrons are not far away. It is logical.'

Jo crept into the cave-room where she had previously talked with the Master. She had found it more by accident than through remembering the way. It was deserted. Everything was just as she last saw it. She picked up the little dull grey box that produced the hypno-sound and pocketed it: it could be useful evidence. Then she turned her attention to the papers on the Master's table and found a star chart; the Master had ringed the Ogrons' planet. Now she looked at the ultra-advanced communications equipment. The controls were helpfully easy to understand. She found the transmitter control, turned it on to full, and spoke into the microphone. 'May Day, May Day. This is an urgent message to Draconians or Earth forces. The Ogrons are using a planet on gallactic co-ordinates 2349 to 6784. Please, anyone who hears this urgent message, inform the authorities of either Earth or

Draconia. May Day, May Day———'

The Master stepped out from the shadows of a corner of the cave room. 'Thank you, Miss Grant.' He came up to the communications equipment and switched it off. 'You see, that was the trap.'

As Jo stepped back her arms were pinioned by an Ogron. Ogrons appeared out of the gloom from all sides.

'What do you mean?' she shouted defiantly. 'You're the one who's trapped. I've given your position away.'

The Master glanced at the papers on his table. 'You mean those planetary co-ordinates I left for you to find, my dear?'

She gasped. 'They were fakes?'

'On the contrary, they're perfectly accurate. But you see this is a short-range transmitter. No one will have picked up your message unless they're within a few hundred miles of this planet.'

Jo felt deflated. 'No one heard me?'

The Master grinned. 'Your friend the Doctor must have heard you. At the moment he's orbiting the planet in a small scout craft. I picked him up on radar some time ago.'

'How do you know it's the Doctor?'

'Who else could it be? You see, when the Doctor arrives we shall be waiting for him. So you've been very useful to me.' The Master turned one of the knobs on his radio equipment. The radio started to emit a regular bleep. 'That's so he won't get lost. He'll think this homing signal comes from you, Miss Grant.'

The Master snapped his fingers. The Ogron holding Jo started to lead her away.

'Oh, by the way, Miss Grant,' said the Master. 'I must congratulate you on escaping, which is exactly what I wanted you to do. But from now on, you'll be kept under guard. You've escaped for the last time, Miss Grant. In fact, I'd say this is the last day of your short and rather eventful life.'

The scout spaceship from Earth made a perfect soft landing on grey sand. Five minutes earlier the pilot had picked up the regular bleeps of what was obviously a homing signal. By manoeuvring the craft, finding the signal sometimes weak and at other times strong, he had narrowed its source to an area of one square mile. Within that area he chose the best possible landing place. From here the party would have to walk, using a pocket receiver to locate in detail where the homing bleeps emanated from.

Alighting from the General's spaceship, the Draconian Prince looked at their inhospitable surroundings. 'I can well understand why neither of us showed any desire to occupy this planet.' He turned to the General. 'In future both Draconia and Earth must maintain constant surveys of these uninhabited planets, to ensure no one is making unlawful use of them.'

'If there *is* a future,' growled the General. 'For all we know, during our absence our two empires may already have wiped each other out.' He caught sight of the Doctor standing some yards away, apparently staring at the sand. 'Doctor, if you could resist day-dreaming we need to complete our mission.'

'Come over here,' called the Doctor. 'Look at this.'

The General and the Prince, followed by the group of Earth soldiers, crossed to where the Doctor was studying huge footprints in the sand.

'According to your records,' said the Doctor, 'one dominant life-form. Let's hope we don't meet it.'

'We are all armed,' the General said confidently.

'We should still hope.' The Doctor turned on the little receiver brought from the spaceship. A regular *bleep-bleep* came from its loudspeaker. By turning the receiver he found the point at which the signal was strongest. 'This way,' he said, leading the party. 'Towards those bushes and rocks.'

As they trudged through the sand, the General asked, 'Doctor, has it occurred to you what we're going to do when we find the source of this signal?'

'No idea, old chap. It depends what we find when we get there.' The Doctor paused, staring at the bushes just ahead.

'What is it?'

'I thought I saw something move. Let's hope it was only a baby lizard.'

The group continued forward until there were rocks and bushes on both sides. The ground was firmer now and they were able to make better progress.

'It occurs to me,' said the Prince, 'that if these lizards are savage they must eat flesh. Therefore they *developed* as flesh eaters, which means there must have been flesh for them to eat. Is it possible, therefore, that the Ogrons have been here a very long time——'

An Ogron suddenly appeared from behind a rock, aiming a heavy blaster gun at the group. 'Stop! Surrender!'

General Williams shouted, 'Take cover!'

Everyone in the party dived behind bushes and rocks as a group of twenty or more Ogrons emerged firing their blaster guns. The Doctor, who had refused the offer of a weapon, found himself behind a stumpy bush with the Draconian Prince. Despite the hail of fire from the Ogrons, the Prince carefully took aim each time before squeezing the trigger of his gun to send a wave of fatal energy into the Ogrons he selected to kill.

The brief battle was terminated by the roar of one of the planet's giant Ogron-eating lizards. Its great head and shoulders suddenly appeared in the Doctor's view as it reared up from behind rocks. The shape of the head, reminiscent of Earth's one-time *tyrannosaurus rex*, with savage shark teeth angled backwards into the mouth, was the same grey colour of the sand and rocks. Different from Earth's most vicious reptile, this lizard's upper limbs were long and mobile, end-ing in enormous seven-fingered claws.

All the Ogrons turned at the sound of the lizard's roaring approach. Unruffled by the creature's appearance, and working strictly to the rules of military opportunism, the Draconian Prince promptly shot dead two Ogrons in the back. The creature roared again, as though it knew the mesmerising effect this had on its victims, leaned forward, picked up a stupefied Ogron and popped him in its mouth. At the sight of their comrade being eaten, the Ogrons dropped their blaster guns and ran for their lives. The lizard, its huge mouth dripping with blood, disappeared from the Doctor's view. The Earth party remained in cover for some moments. From the distance they could hear the screams and cries of the retreating Ogrons and the roars of the lizard in pursuit.

General Williams emerged from his hiding place. He was badly shaken by what he had just seen, but quickly recovered himself. He looked at two dead Earth soldiers. 'Which way, Doctor?'

'Straight ahead, General.' The Doctor looked at the two dead soldiers. 'I'm very sorry.'

'We shall take them back with us,' said the General. 'That is our custom.'

The party went forward.

The Master spoke deferentially into the microphone of his communications equipment. 'Yes, I admit there have been setbacks. But I have now lured the Doctor to my trap. With your help we shall have no further difficulties. I await your arrival with the greatest pleasure and will meet your ship at the landing place.'

He switched off the transmitter. An Ogron entered.

'Well, where's the Doctor?' asked the Master.

'The big lizard came.'

'And I suppose you ran like rabbits?' The Master turned to leave the cave-room. 'You will answer for this to your masters.'

The Ogron looked startled. '*They* are coming?'

'Yes,' the Master hissed in the Ogron's face. 'They're on their way. Fortunately I can now dispense with your assistance.' The Master hurried away to meet the new arrivals.

'*They* are coming,' the Ogron said to himself. '*They* are coming!' The significance of this finally penetrated his tiny mind. He hurried away into a gloomy corridor, very worried.

'That sound,' said the Draconian Prince. 'Another ship is surely landing.'

The party paused to listen. By the approaching roar of rocket motors it was clearly a spaceship landing fairly close to them.

General Williams suggested, 'Perhaps someone else picked up your young friend's May Day message.'

'Perhaps,' said the Doctor thoughtfully. 'I wonder ...'

'What is it?' asked the General.

The Doctor shrugged. 'I just had a feeling, some kind of premonition. Anyway, let's press on.' He held up the little receiver. The bleeps were very strong now. 'It seems we must go through this valley. I suggest we all be on our guard.'

As they went forward again the ground on both sides rose in big rock-covered shoulders. Some distance ahead were cliffs and the Doctor thought he could see the mouths of caves. Between them and the cliffs lay huge boulders, as though some giant had cast pebbles along the floor of the valley.

The General looked up at the sides of the valley. 'That's where we should be, Doctor, with a commanding view——'

The Master suddenly stepped out from behind a boulder a few yards ahead of the party. 'Hello, Doctor! There you are at long last!'

General Williams raised an arm to halt his party. 'Surrender or you will be shot down!' He aimed his blaster gun to fire.

'No!' said the Doctor. 'He's unarmed.'

'Thank you, Doctor,' called the Master. 'Always the good pacifist. I am unarmed, but not alone. I've brought some old friends along to meet you.'

As he spoke a Dalek glided out from behind the boulder, its deadly firing weapon trained on the Doctor.

'Don't do anything rash, Doctor,' shouted the Master. 'Look around you.'

The Doctor looked up at the rising ground. On all sides Daleks had appeared.

'What are these machines?' asked General Williams. 'He says they're your friends.'

'The Master's little joke,' replied the Doctor. 'No, they're not machines, not exactly. They are what remains of one of the greatest species of the galaxy. Unfortunately they turned to war, a terrible conflict of nuclear weapons. It backfired on them. Through mutation they started to decay. Realising that soon only their brains would be left, they devised these mobile domes that you see now all around us. In their bitterness they became the most vicious, ruthless creatures ever to live in Space. They are my most deadly enemies.'

'Then they must be destroyed,' said General Williams. He called to his soldiers, 'Open fire!'

Before the Earth soldiers could raise their weapons, the Daleks had fired on them. Williams tried to raise his blaster gun but the Doctor knocked it from his hands.

'It's no good, General. We must submit.'

The Doctor, General Williams and the Draconian Prince were led into the main meeting cave of the

Ogrons' stronghold. A Dalek was waiting. It addressed the Doctor in a harsh, mechanical monotone.

'Doctor, you are in the power of the Daleks. You will be taken to our planet and exterminated.' Even the Ogrons present quavered at the deathly sound of the Dalek's voice.

'If I may speak,' said the Master. 'This man has been my enemy as well as yours. He does not fear death. I wish him to suffer a worse punishment. Leave him with me so that he can see the results of the war which my cunning and skill has created. Let him see the galaxy, including that planet Earth he loved so well, in ruins. Then exterminate him.'

The Dalek turned towards the Master. 'He will remain your prisoner until the war is concluded. Then you will bring him to us. We shall return to our planet now and prepare the army of the Daleks.' The Dalek glided away down a corridor into the darkness beyond.

'I suppose I should thank you,' the Doctor told the Master. 'You seem to have saved my life.'

'Not for long, Doctor. It will be a very short war.' The Master turned to the Ogron guards. 'Take him away.'

The Doctor was put into the cell with Jo, who promptly flung her arms round him. General Williams and the Prince were placed in the adjacent cell. The hole Jo had dug was filled in with rocks.

'These Dalek creatures,' the Prince spoke through the bars. 'Why do they wish to set my people against Earth?'

'Because war will mean the end of both empires,' explained the Doctor. 'The Daleks will emerge as supreme rulers.'

'Doctor,' Jo said excitedly, tugging at his sleeve, 'I've got one of those things. Look! I stole it when I escaped for a while.' She produced the dull grey box, keeping it well out of sight of the Ogron guard on the other side of the bars.

'What is it?'

'You know,' she whispered. 'It makes people see things.' She tilted her head to indicate the Ogron guard. 'You could use it to frighten *him*!'

'He'd only run away,' said the Doctor. 'We'd still be locked in.' An idea formed in his mind. 'But there is something we might do with very fine adjustment ...' He started to inspect the controls. In an undertone he whispered through the bars to their fellow prisoners. 'General, if we get out of here, and Miss Grant and I create a diversion, could you two find your way back to the ship?'

'Naturally,' said the General.

'Good. I want you to take off immediately and get the truth to your respective governments.'

The Draconian Prince put his snout close to the bars. 'I shall stay and help you.'

'No, Your Highness. We need you to convince the Emperor,' said the Doctor, making final adjustments to the controls on the hypno-sound device. 'Incidentally, Jo, I take it that the TARDIS is here somewhere?'

She nodded. 'I could lead you there—I think.'

'Excellent. Now all of you, close your eyes and block your ears. If you don't it could be rather unpleasant for you.' The Doctor went forward to the bars and called to the Ogron guard. 'How long are you going to keep us stuck in here? Hey, I'm speaking to you.'

The guard lumbered forward menacingly. 'You keep quiet or I fill mouth with fist.'

'Charming,' said the Doctor. 'Well, let's see how you feel about this.' He turned on the hypno-sound device to full strength.

The Ogron guard stopped, eyes dilated. The strange sound made his mind reel. As he stared, the Doctor's form on the other side of the bars became blurred, then re-formed as a Dalek.

'Open the gate,' the Doctor told him, imitating a Dalek voice. 'Open the gate or I shall exterminate you.'

The Ogron tried to assemble his thoughts. 'Master say keep gate locked.'

'We are the masters of the Master,' the Dalek looked menacingly at him through the bars. 'Open or I shall exterminate you. Exterminate, *exterminate!*'

Shaking with fear the Ogron produced a massive key and turned it in the lock. Then he fled in terror.

The Doctor and Jo stepped out to freedom. The Doctor took the key, unlocked the gate to the other cell, went inside and touched the General and the Prince on their shoulders. 'You can open your eyes now.'

They looked at the Doctor in astonishment. 'What did you do?' asked the General.

'Put it down to magic,' the Doctor grinned. He showed them the hypno-sound device. 'This little thing almost caused you two to blow each other to smithereens. I'd love to explain how it works but there isn't time. We've got to find the Master.' He turned to Jo. 'Where did you send your May Day message from?'

Jo looked down the corridor where the terrified Ogron had run. 'I *think* it was that way.'

'Try your best to remember, Jo,' said the Doctor. 'A lot depends on it.'

The Master was using his transmitting equipment to talk to the departing Daleks whose spaceship was now in flight. 'You have no need to worry. The Doctor is safe in my hands. When I bring him to you, he will be a broken man.'

A Dalek voice answered over the loudspeaker. 'Do not fail the Daleks. We are about to enter hyper-drive and return to our planet. Do not fail the Daleks.'

The Master replied, 'I shall not fail you.'

Nothing further came over the loudspeaker so he presumed that was the end of the conversation. The Daleks were not given to the normal pleasantries of bidding farewell. He switched off the transmitter. 'Stupid tin boxes,' he said to himself. 'We'll see who really rules the galaxy once this war has ruined Earth and Draconia.' Imitating a Dalek voice he said, '*Exterminate*—indeed!'

The Ogron guard from the cells stumbled into the cave-room. He was too terrified and confused to speak, but stood there panting.

'What's wrong with you?' said the Master. 'Why aren't you guarding the prisoners?'

The Ogron caught his breath. 'The Dalek sent me away.'

'Don't be stupid,' said the Master. 'There are no Daleks here now. They've all left. Go back to your post and stop imagining things.' As he said the word *imagining*, a terrible thought crossed his mind. He searched quickly among his equipment for the hypno-sound device.

The Ogron persisted, 'Dalek said open the gate.'

'And you, of course, opened it.' The Master tried to conceal any panic in his voice. 'Get the others. I want them here at once.'

The Ogron looked blank. 'The other Daleks?'

The Master closed his eyes and tried to keep a grip on his sanity. 'No, you stupid moron, the other Ogrons. Big, idiot imbeciles like yourself. Got the idea?'

As understanding dawned, the Ogron's face cracked into a grin. 'Other Ogrons like me.' Then he frowned, his mind troubled again. 'Why you want them?'

'I thought we could all have afternoon tea together. Now go!'

The escaping prisoners had arrived at the brightly-lit

area where previously Jo had seen the Ogron make a food sacrifice. The Doctor looked up at the drawing, intensely interested.

'Fascinating,' he murmured.

'I think the Ogrons worship it,' explained Jo.

'Not surprising,' said the Doctor. 'They're probably more frightened of those giant lizards than they are of the Daleks. A pity we can't stay here long enough to learn more about their culture. Now Jo, where did you go from here?'

She looked at the corridors leading in various directions. 'That's the way out of here,' she said emphatically, pointing to a wide corridor. 'But that wasn't the way I went.'

'Even so,' said the Doctor, 'that's the way for you two—General—Your Highness. Get back to your peoples as fast as you can. Make sure they never contemplate war again.'

The Draconian Prince stepped forward. 'I wish to thank you on behalf of the Draconian Empire.'

'And I on behalf of Earth,' said General Williams. 'May you live a long life——'

The Doctor cut in with a smile. 'Yes, yes indeed, but I think we should all hurry now. Goodbye. Come on, Jo, lead me to the TARDIS.'

He hurried Jo away.

The TARDIS stood in the corner where Jo had seen it before. When the Doctor and Jo entered the Master's cave it seemed to be completely deserted.

'There it is,' Jo pointed excitedly. 'Have you got the key?'

'Right here, Jo.' The Doctor fished in his pocket.

As they approached the TARDIS, Jo asked, 'Where are we going this time, Doctor?'

'I should think that's pretty obvious,' he said, about to insert the key in the lock of the old-fashioned London police box. 'We're going to——'

The Master stepped out from behind the TARDIS,

a blaster gun pointed at the Doctor. 'I don't think you're going anywhere, Doctor. I believe you have some property of mine, something Miss Grant stole when she was in here before.' He raised his voice. 'Ogrons forward, please.'

From all sides Ogrons appeared, shuffling out of the gloom.

'Are you referring to this?' asked the Doctor as he produced the hypno-sound device. 'A most ingenious gadget, if I may say so. You could cause a lot of trouble with it.'

As he spoke the Doctor turned the device on to full volume. The sudden sound sent the Master reeling backwards, clutching his ears and dropping his blaster gun. The Doctor spun round to face the encircling Ogrons.

The terrible sound roaring through their midget minds, the Ogrons saw the shape of the Doctor blurr before their eyes. Then he re-formed into the thing they feared most—a giant, Ogron-eating lizard, rearing up its great head and roaring at them. They turned and fled, fighting and stumbling over each other to run away.

The Master regained his senses. 'Come back!' he screamed at the Ogrons. 'There's nothing to be frightened of. It's an illusion.' Then he saw his blaster gun on the ground, reached down to retrieve it.

The Doctor got there first and picked up the gun. The Master stepped back, hands raised, his face contorted in fear. 'Are you going to kill me?'

With his free hand, the Doctor unlocked the door to the TARDIS. 'Go inside, Jo.'

She hesitated. 'Doctor, you couldn't, not in cold blood ...'

'Go inside,' he repeated.

Jo went into the safety of the TARDIS.

'Well,' said the Master, 'you only have to squeeze the trigger.'

'You know that I couldn't kill you,' said the Doctor. 'Perhaps I should take you prisoner and return you to serve your prison sentence on Earth. But there's something more important for me to do at the moment.'

'What's that?'

'To go after the Daleks, of course. Stand well back.'

The Master, hands still raised, walked slowly backwards. 'This far enough?' His old spirit was already returning and a smile touched his lips.

'That's far enough for safety.' The Doctor hurled the blaster gun into a distant corner, well away from the Master's reach.

The Master grinned. 'Perhaps we shall meet again, Doctor.'

'Yes, perhaps we shall.'

The Doctor closed the door of the TARDIS. The Master watched as it dematerialised. Then he went back to his big table and started to collect his star charts and other papers. 'Oh well,' he said to himself, 'there's always tomorrow.'

STAY ON

Here are details of other exciting TARGET titles.
If you cannot obtain these books from your
local bookshop, or newsagent, write to the
address below listing the titles you would like
and enclosing cheque or postal order — *not*
currency — including 15p to cover packing
and postage, and 8p for each additional copy.

TARGET BOOKS
Wyndham Publications Ltd.,
123 King Street,
London, W6 9JG

If you enjoyed this book and would like to have information sent you about other TARGET titles, write to the address below.

You will also receive:
A FREE TARGET BADGE!
Based on the TARGET BOOKS symbol—see front cover of this book—this attractive three-colour badge, pinned to your blazer-lapel or jumper, will excite the interest and comment of all your friends!

and you will be further entitled to:
FREE ENTRY INTO THE TARGET DRAW!
All you have to do is cut off the coupon beneath, write on it your name and address in *block capitals*, and pin it to your letter. Twice a year, in June, and December, coupons will be drawn 'from the hat' and the winner will receive a complete year's set of TARGET books.

Write to:

TARGET BOOKS,
Tandem Publishing Ltd.,
123 King Street,
London W6 9JG

If you live in New Zealand, write to:
TARGET BOOKS
Whitcoulls Ltd.,
111, Cashel Street,
Christchurch

If you live in South Africa, write to:

TARGET BOOKS,
Purnell & Sons,
505, C.N.A. Building,
110, Commissioner Street,
Johannesburg

If you live in Australia, write to:

TARGET BOOKS,
Rical Enterprises Pty. Ltd.,
Daking House,
11, Rawson Place,
Sydney, N.S. Wales 2000

———————————cut here———————————

Full name...

Address...

....

....

Age..

PLEASE ENCLOSE A SELF-ADDRESSED ENVELOPE WITH YOUR COUPON.